Edward A. Plater

The Holy Coat of Treves

A sketch of its history, cultus, and solemn expositions ; with notes on relics

generally

Edward A. Plater

The Holy Coat of Treves
A sketch of its history, cultus, and solemn expositions ; with notes on relics generally

ISBN/EAN: 9783741189081

Manufactured in Europe, USA, Canada, Australia, Japa

Cover: Foto ©Andreas Hilbeck / pixelio.de

Manufactured and distributed by brebook publishing software
(www.brebook.com)

Edward A. Plater

The Holy Coat of Treves

THE

HOLY COAT OF TRÈVES.

A SKETCH

*Of its History, Cultus, and solemn Expositions ; with
Notes on Relics generally.*

WITH ILLUSTRATIONS.

" *Erat autem Tunica inconsutilis, desuper*
contexta per totum—JOAN. XIX. 23.

BY

EDWARD A. PLATER.

London :

R. WASHBOURNE,

18, PATERNOSTER ROW.

1891.

[Entered at Stationers' Hall.]

Willems (traduit par Furcy Raynaud); " La Sainte Relique de Trèves," par L'Abbé Bénard of Nancy; " Wallfahrt zum hl. Rock in Trier," by Domvikar Joseph Hulley; " Die Wallfahrt nach Trier," (1844) by Joseph Görres; and " Geschichte des hl. Rockes," by Professor Marx.

He wishes also to acknowledge his obligation to Mr. Osmund Seager for his pamphlet on the Exposition of 1844, and to the Rev. R. T. Clarke, S.J., for his admirable article in the " Month" magazine of October, 1891.

WEST KENSINGTON,
    28th October, 1891.

TABLE OF CONTENTS.

—◆—

THE

HOLY COAT OF TRÈVES.

CHAPTER I.

INTRODUCTORY.

DURING the late summer of last year, in the course
of a holiday tour in Germany, the writer first made
acquaintance with the old-world city of Trèves; and
if the shortness of his stay was a disappointment,
he was at least encouraged to look forward to a
second visit, under circumstances of unusual interest,
in the year to follow. For rumours were already
afloat of the proposed solemn Exposition of the great
Relic with which the name of Trèves has been associated for so many centuries, the " seamless Tunic of
our Lord."

Forty-six years had elapsed since Trèves last held
high fête in sight of the object of its veneration,
and all city and diocese were overjoyed at learning
that its Bishop was just then engaged, with the

Chapter of his Cathedral, and with the assistance of trusted experts, in conducting a minute and searching scrutiny of the Relic, with a view to the re-establishment of its authenticity, the clearing up of all possible suggestions of doubt, and the confirmation of the immemorial tradition. This course had been adopted in conformity with the usage of the Church, and with the caution enjoined by the Council of Trent for the safe-guarding of Holy Relics, and the avoidance of abuses. But there were further reasons to recommend it. On the occasion of the last solemn Exposition of the Relic in 1844, in spite of the profound impression created, and of the marvels, material as well as spiritual, then effected, various unfavorable criticisms were directed against the authenticity of the Holy Coat. In one or two such instances, certainly, the authors were men of repute and learning, and known to be sound in the Faith. The difficulties of such men claimed respect; but there were others, for the most part men of known hostility to the Church, and sided with these were certain Catholics with a leaning towards Rationalism. Two of the foremost, Czerski, an ecclesiastic of Posen, and Ronge, a suspended priest of Breslau, subsequently seceded from the Church.

The formal examination of the Relic commenced on the 5th July, 1890, and was continued until the

11th; when, enveloped in silk, and cased in fourfold coverings of wood and lead, it was re-consigned to its marble chamber beneath the high altar.

The records of each days' examination were separately recorded, and the procès verbaux from· day to day were signed by the Bishop, by the Coadjutor Bishop, Mgr. Feiten, and by the members of the Commission; the result of the scrutiny being to confirm in the minds of all present the inviolable truth of the tradition of the Church of Trèves.

Alluding to this scrutiny in his Pastoral to the faithful of his Diocese, Mgr. Korum thus concludes: " I therefore regard it an imperative duty of my charge as Bishop to declare solemnly in the sight of God and men our deep conviction that the Holy Robe preserved at Trèves is the true seamless Tunic of our Saviour, and that my venerable predecessors have been neither deceivers nor deceived."

From a learned work on the history and archæology of the Holy Coat by Dr. Willems, we gather that for many years past the voice of the Catholics of Germany has from time to time expressed its longing for the privilege of venerating the Relic so long hidden from their sight. But that voice was at length to find a fitting mouthpiece when, at the Congress of the Catholics of Germany in 1887, a venerable prelate*

* The Bishop of Luxembourg.

rose among the assembled bishops, clergy, and laity, and turning to the Bishop of Trèves, solemnly requested him, in the name of Catholic Germany, to afford them once again the opportunity of venerating in public Exposition the Holy Coat of Trèves, the seamless Tunic of our Blessed Lord. The incident was wholly unexpected. The huge assembly burst into a roar of acclamation, and their enthusiasm was only checked when Mgr. Korum, taken by surprise and profoundly moved by the fervour of the assembled Fathers, at length rose to address them. Doubtless he bore in mind the events of the past half-century, the political and religious strife which had transformed the face of Europe, and the struggles in which the Church had been engaged: times so inappropriate to the public manifestation of that Holy Robe, the symbol of the unity of Christ's Church and of the peace of our Blessed Lord. With such thoughts, in an address of touching solemnity, the Bishop inquires: " Are then the happier times recurring? I cannot of myself decide. The future is not in man's hands. Times and seasons are God's to determine: but of this I can venture to assure you, my brothers, my children, that should the coming times be judged favorable, and life be spared to me, all Catholic Germany shall be witness of the veneration, the loving honour in which its sacred deposit is held by the City of Trèves."

To many of those who attended the recent solemnity at Trèves, one reflection must have forcibly occurred, the *suitability of the place* as the home in which the Relic has sojourned these long centuries. The startling reminders of the Empire of old Rome which unexpectedly confront a stranger—the Porta Nigra, the Amphitheatre, the Basilica—make him stand amazed, and perhaps carry him back in thought to early school days, as they did the writer, and to his first struggles over Cæsar's Commentaries; and while remembering the troubles caused him by these "Treviri," and the "Civitas Trevirorum," he may also call to mind that their conquest gave no little trouble too to Julius Cæsar,—so far back as between 58 and 51 B.C.,—who found them already a powerful and highly civilized people.

This would seem to constitute a respectable antiquity, but far more is claimed for them by the old tradition of their Eastern origin, which assigns their foundation to one Trebeta, son of Ninus, the Assyrian king, and is embodied in the lines conspicuous upon the old Rathaus:

Ante Romam Treviris stetit annis mille trecentis;

Perstet, et æterna pace fruatur.—Amen.

Nor in its Christian aspect is the antiquity of Trèves less remarkable. Its first preachers of the faith are held to have received their commission at

the hands of the Prince of the Apostles; and to
these first bishops, sent by him—St. Eucharius,
St. Valerius, and St. Maternus — the Church of
Trèves traces its origin.* In a sketch of the lives
of these first Apostles, written about the year 900,†
allusion is made to their having been received by
one Albana, widow of a Senator, who lodged them
in her villa, upon the site of which the Church of
St. Eucharius and St. Matthias was erected later on;
and there it was that the Christian Mysteries were
first celebrated. Recent excavations in the Cemetery
of St. Matthias go to confirm this account: they
disclose the remains of a Roman villa of the time
of the Flavians, with ancient Christian tombs against
its walls, and the traces of a large chamber or
oratory. As the great antiquarian Canon Wilmowski
remarks, "Mother Earth had not failed to render up
proofs which would be sought in vain from archives
which had perished in the strife of ages."

All ancient writers bear witness to the great numbers
of the Christians here in the third Century, and to
the crowds of martyrs produced by the Church of

---

* The staff given by St. Peter to St. Eucharius—by which St. Maternus,
his companion, is said to have been brought back to life—is still preserved
among the treasures of Trèves, and authorities tell us that it would be used
by a Pope celebrating Solemn Mass in that Cathedral.

† Other mention of these Apostles is found in Life of St. Maximus, VIII
Cent.; in a document of Archbp. Numerian about 664; in an inscription by
Bp. Cyril in 1455; and other early writings.

Trèves during the persecutions under Dioclesian and his successors. Here St. Helena with her son Constantine held their court; and after her conversion she bequeathed her palace to be the nucleus of the Cathedral as we nôw see it. Here St. Athanasius—banished from his see at Alexandria—took refuge for the space of two years: and he recounts having to celebrate in a half-built church because of the throng of Christians. Other great saints have trodden its streets: its stones have been worn by the footsteps of St. Jerome, Doctor of the Church; St. Ambrose, the great Archbishop of Milan, and St. Martin, the Thaumaturge of Gaul. Two score and more of saints, and many martyrs, are counted in its line of bishops. St. Eucharius, its first bishop, St. Agritius, and St. Nicetius are amongst that company, and rest within its walls: and the visits of Sovereign Pontiffs, St. Leo the IX. and Pope Eugenius the III., have added lustre to its history.

Hence in both aspects, Pagan and Christian, the old city shared pre-eminence with Rome. As in Pagan times it had been the central city and great seat of government this side the Alps, so in the Christian kingdom it was to become, after Rome, the recognized Mother Church of Central Europe; and a recent writer* supplies the fact that in our own days a Bishop of Trèves, the saint-like William Arnoldi, shared with Pope Pius the IX. the glory of suffering for Christ's sake.

---

* O. Seager.

CHAPTER II.

RELICS.

FOR those unacquainted with the teaching of the Catholic Church, who may have hitherto trusted to the chatter of the day for their notions upon the veneration which Catholics accord to saints and their relics—for such as these some plain statement of the Church's teaching is here requisite, if only for the better understanding of the phenomenon presented to the world's sight by the recent spectacle at Trèves —of the tens of thousands of men and women, of all classes of society, rich and poor, simple and learned, high-born and obscure, laity of every calling, clergy, bishops, from all parts of Europe—nay from America —converging, in ceaseless procession of six weeks' duration, upon an unpretending German town, which, whatever its former glories, now lies quite apart from the world's great highways, and lays no claim to rivalry with the well-known centres of life and industry, of civilization and government.

By the term " Relics" is denoted the bodies of the saints, fragments of their bodies, and articles which they have used, or which pertain to them. In a still more eminent degree is the term applicable to articles or portions of articles pertaining to our Saviour and His Blessed Mother, which naturally take the highest rank.

Upon the propriety and utility of the veneration of relics the teaching of the Church is plain, and it is a simple matter of faith.

The Council of Trent—following upon the teaching of former Councils, and notably of the second Council of Nicea—in its 25th Session solemnly approves of the veneration of relics, and condemns those who teach that such veneration is unfitting and useless.*

The Church has ever honoured the bodies of those who sleep in Christ, a practice following naturally and necessarily from our Lord's pledge and assurance of the resurrection of the body. She also specially venerates the relics of her saints, His chosen servants. For the Scripture teaching we are referred, in the Old Testament, to the dead body of the man brought to life by contact with the bones of the Prophet Eliseus ; and, in the New, to the sick healed by the handkerchiefs and napkins taken from the body of St. Paul. The early Christians so held from the infancy of the Church. Thus, they collected the bones of the martyr, St. Ignatius (A.D. 107), which were

---

* Omnino damnandas esse, prout jam pridem eos damnavit, et nunc etiam "damnat Ecclesia."—Conc. Trid., Sess. xxv.

conveyed to Antioch "as a priceless treasure bequeathed to that Holy Church by the grace that was in the martyr." Thus they exhumed the ashes of St. Polycarp's body (A.D. 167)—it had been burned by the Jews to hinder their venerating it—which they describe "as more costly than precious stones, and refined beyond all gold." Thus, too, when St. Cyprian was about to be beheaded, they cast towels and napkins before him to save his blood.

To take the language of the Fathers. St. Ephrem, the oldest Father of the Oriental Church : " I entreat you, holy martyrs, who have suffered so much for the Lord, that you would intercede for us with Him, that He bestow His grace on us."* Again, "See how the relics of the martyrs still breathe, . . . For the Deity dwells in the bones of the martyrs, and by His power and presence miracles are wrought." St. John Chrysostom: "That which neither riches nor gold can effect, the relics of martyrs can. Gold never dispelled diseases, nor warded off death : but the bones of the martyrs have done both ; in the days of our forefathers the former happened, the latter in our own."† St. Basil sends from Cappadocia relics of St. Dionisius to St. Ambrose at Milan, at the earnest request of the latter.‡ St. Ambrose

---

* Encom. in SS. Mart T. iii., p. 251.
† Homil. lxii., S. Drosidis Mart. T. v. P. 882.
‡ Ad Ambros. Mediol. Ep. cxcvii.

translates the bodies of SS. Gervasius and Protasius to his Basilica, and on their passage a blind man recovers his sight.* St. Augustine in many Homilies on the martyrs recounts the miracles wrought by their relics, and especially instances cases at the tomb of St. Stephen. St. Cyril of Jerusalem says, " There is a power latent in even the bodies of the just." Other Fathers, too, of the fourth and fifth centuries witness to the miracles wrought through the instrumentality of the relics of the saints, and to the general belief of the Faithful of their times.

Plentiful indeed—both in the Old and New Testa-ments—are the instances of a Divine Power, working under the external covering of material and inanimate things. Among others, it is obvious to point to the account of Naaman being directed to wash seven times in the Jordan ; to the tree cast into the waters to sweeten them ; to Eliseus throwing the meal into the pot of poisonous herbs; to the same prophet's striking the waters of Jordan with the mantle of Elias, and dividing them ; and to his casting salt into the water of the impure spring. We may point also, to our Saviour's making clay to anoint the eyes of the man born blind ; to His bidding St. Peter catch a fish to obtain the money for tribute; and to St. Peter's very shadow being sought for by the sick and afflicted.

---

* Epistol. Lib. vii. Ep. 56.

St. Thomas Aquinas lays down, "Therefore we ought to venerate the relics of the saints in fitting honour of their memory, and especially their bodies which were the temples of the Holy Spirit inhabiting, and working in them ; which are also to be configured to the body of Christ by a glorious resurrection. Moreover, God Himself has been pleased to honour such relics by working miracles in their presence."* In the same place he quotes St. Augustine, who says, "The bodies of the Saints, and especially the Relics of the blessed Martyrs, they being members of Christ, are to be sincerely held in honour. Anyone holding the contrary opinion is rather a follower of Eunomius and Vigilantius than of Christ."†

Nearly half-a-century ago, an eminent author, whose memory is revered wherever the English tongue is heard, and indeed throughout the civilized world, the late Cardinal Newman,—then on the eve of his submission to the Catholic Church,—writing on the development of Christian doctrine, pursues a line of thought, which had best be given in his own words. He speaks of "A characteristic principle of Christianity, whether in the East or in the West, which is at present both a special stumbling block and a subject of scoffing with Protestants and free-thinkers

---

* S. Thom. Aq. Pars. lii. Qu. xxv., Art 6.
† Lib. de Eccl. dogm.

of every shade and colour: I mean," he says, " the devotion which both Greeks and Latins show towards bones, blood, the heart, the hair, etc., etc.; and the miraculous powers which they often ascribe to them. Now, the principle from which these beliefs and usages proceed is the doctrine that matter is susceptible of grace, or capable of a union with a Divine presence and influence."

Again : " Christianity began by considering matter as a creature of God, and in itself ' very good.' It taught that matter, as well as spirit, had become corrupt, in the instance of Adam ; and it contemplated its recovery. It taught that the Highest had taken a portion of that corrupt mass upon Himself, in order to the sanctification of the whole ; that, as a first fruits of His purpose, He had purified from all sin that very portion of it which He took into His Eternal Person, and thereunto had taken it from a Virgin Womb, which He had filled with the abundance of His Spirit. . . . . It taught that the Highest had in that flesh died upon the Cross, and that His blood had an expiatory power ; moreover that He had risen again in that flesh, and had carried that flesh with Him into Heaven, and that from that flesh, glorified and deified in Him, He never would be divided. As a first consequence of these awful doctrines comes that of the resurrection of the bodies of His saints, and of their future glorification with Him; next that of the sanctity of their relics. . . .

And they were all objects of offence or of scorn to philosophers, priests, or populace of the day. . . . The one great topic of preaching with apostles and evangelists was the resurrection of Christ and of all mankind after Him; but when the philosophers of Athens heard St. Paul, 'some mocked, and others contemptuously put aside the doctrine.'" . . . . Again: "According to the old Paganism both the educated and vulgar held corpses and sepulchres in aversion. . . . . 'When deaths were Judaical,' says the writer who goes under the name of St. Basil, 'corpses were an abomination; when death is for Christ, the relics of saints are precious.' It was anciently said to the priests and Nazarites: ' If anyone shall touch a corpse, he shall be unclean till evening, and he shall wash his garment'; now, on the contrary, if anyone shall touch a martyr's bones, by reason of the grace dwelling in the body, he receives some participation in his sanctity," &c.

Elsewhere he says: "The store of relics is inexhaustible; they are multiplied through all lands, and each particle of each has in it at least a dormant, perhaps an energetic virtue of supernatural operation."*

---

* Id Lect. "Present position," No. VII.

So much, then, may here suffice upon the doctrine
of the veneration to be paid to relics in general:—
·(1) The Church teaches it as an Article of the Faith.
(2) The warrant of her teaching is manifest in Holy
Scripture. (3) In the mind of the Faithful it has
been ever accepted, both intellectually and devo-
tionally, and embodied in their daily practise from
the apostolic age till now.

But in considering the devotion to be paid to particular relics, it by no means follows that the Church
condemns those who may doubt their authenticity
in this or that particular instance. Here is purely a
matter of human testimony, whether perpetuated by
the evidence of trustworthy documents, or by the
continuous tradition of men upon whose good faith
there is every reason to rely.

Abuses have no doubt occurred in all ages; and
surprising too have been the instances of their provi-
dential exposure: still the Church has ever exercised
an unceasing care to avoid them, in the jealous
precautions on which she has insisted. Some of
these it may be worth while to indicate here. The
fourth Lateran Council in 1215 (Can. 62) laid down
stringent rules to guard the authenticity of relics.
The Council of Trent (Sess. xxv.) renews these precautions and desires, *(vehementer cupit)* that where
abuses have crept in they shall be wholly eradicated,

and all superstitions banished: moreover, that bishops shall only decide in the case of *unusual* relics *(insolitos)*, after careful consultation with theologians, and, if . necessary, with the metropolitan and other bishops of the province in Council assembled; with this further proviso, besides, that nothing new or hitherto strange to the custom of the Church shall be decreed without the sanction of the Sovereign Pontiff. The same anxiety is manifest in the decisions of other Councils, and of Synods, both provincial and diocesan; as, at Frankfort in 734; at Thionville in 805; at Aix la Chapelle (itself a wonderful storehouse of relics) in 789; at Mainz, under Charlemagne, in 813; at Poitiers in 1100; at Magdeburg in 1362.

Where else then shall saints and martyrs look to find such jealous custody for their mortal remnants as in her hands whose children they were in life? Devotion to relics, whether sacred or secular, means *loyalty* to the persons whom they represent, and, apart from any hypothesis of a Divine protection,— we may trust that the loving instincts of disciples and spiritual children, not to mention the pride of country, district, race,—would form no feeble safe-guard to such loyalty and integrity.

At the same time it may be submitted, that although the Church does not propose a particular relic as a matter of faith, or anathematize those who venture to doubt its authenticity, still the individual would hardly escape the imputation of rashness, of presumption and irreverence, who should venture wantonly and without grave reasons to oppose his personal opinion to the traditions and devout belief of generations of his fellow men—no whit less jealous than himself of the suspicion of error, whether of accident or by design.

One can hardly imagine a Catholic passing over as unimportant, still less rejecting, every doctrine which happens not to be "de Fide." This would imply sheer indifference to being in harmony with the Church (as Fr. Faber says), and a purpose of only turning the corner of formal heresy by an adroit and perilous nicety. Some doctrines are so certain, that it is doubtful whether they are "of faith" or not: others are "proximæ fidei"; others, again, are certain "de fide Ecclesiastica"; others are met with in the Offices of the Church, or have been accepted by canonized saints, or find expression in indulgenced devotions. What would be thought— to take an extreme case—of a Catholic who should deny that any relics of the Cross were genuine? Such an one might be well reminded that, while steering clear of formal heresy, it is possible to incur no less than twenty-three distinct censures of the Church, of which, "close upon heresy"—

"schismatical"—"blasphemous"—"erroneous," are specimens. No amount of sanction by the Church of God, even the very least degree which she ever accords, can be a light or mean thing in the sight and consciences of her children.*

A passage from a recent lecture by Fr. Gavin, S.J., may from its appositeness be added here: "Many things the Pope does from the fullness of his Apostolic authority which do not come within the range of his Infallibility. And yet no one would deny that, in those solemn acts, the Sovereign Pontiff had the protection of his Lord and Master. If we contended that the protection of God extended over the Holy Father merely when he spoke ' ex Cathedra,' we almost ceased to be Catholics."

In the multitude of comments which this subject has always elicited from outside, misrepresentations of every form would be expected. The scope of this short inquiry will scarcely allow of any lengthened notice of them; but one common misconception may be mentioned. It is, that Popes have guaranteed the authenticity of relics; and that such guarantee involves the exercise of infallibility. This is absolutely untrue. The authenticity of a particular relic falls under no precept of Catholic faith. For such concurrence as Popes may grant in particular cases, the Holy See

* Faber, Essay on Beatification, &c.

is necessarily dependent upon the wisdom and dili-
gence of the commission of " pious and learned men"
whom it has trusted with the work of investigation.
Upon their trustworthy decision the Pope is pleased
to permit that those who believe in the relics should
have the opportunity of showing them public veneration, and he rewards with Indulgences their piety
and devotion. Moreover, insomuch as this veneration
of relics is in its nature relative, being directed to
the relics for the saint's sake, and from the saint
passing on to Him, the King of Saints, there remains
a true and meritorious act of devotion—wholly apart
from any infallible assurance of authenticity.

Theologians have laid down the degree of certitude
necessary to establish the title to veneration. One
or two may be here sufficient. The high authority
of Benedict the XIV. is quoted as requiring a *moral*
certitude (not a metaphysical or physical)—and such
a moral certitude, founded on trustworthy testimony of
men, as we are content to rely upon in most affairs
of life.

On this principle, the learned Bollandist Papebroch
(himself regarded as the most merciless of critics)
thus comments : " In the matter of relics," he says,
" we should rely rather upon a pious belief, than
upon our personal knowledge that they can be distinctly traced from hand to hand."

A passage from a work by Cardinal Manning, although upon the wider subject of Christianity and revealed religion, may appropriately be referred to here. His Eminence writes: " If nothing can be received on trust, why should I believe in the existence of Byzantium, or in the invasion of Britain by Julius Cæsar? Human society and the most vital truths in the life of man come to us on hearsay. But the hearsay of the Christian world . . . is affirmed and believed to be divine, etc. . . . The testimony of twelve men laid the foundation of the testimony of the whole Christian world." He continues: " Schlegel has well said that the witness of the Christian world is the maximum of evidence in history. If this be not a motive of credibility sufficient to make a prudent man responsible, what can be so, short of a separate revelation to each man who is pleased to doubt."*

Does not this account for the importance attached to the " Traditions of the Churches "? not merely because of the worldly respectability of such and such men (or generations of men), but because they have lived their lives in the "fear of God," the very condition and guarantee, as well as the " beginning" of " wisdom."

See how the devotion to relics is conspicuous in

---

* Religio Viatoris, pp. 55, 56.

the Lives of Canonized Saints. I take the first
volumes that come to hand. St. Ignatius, after his
first year at Manresa, starts on a pilgrimage to
Jerusalem ; he gets the permission and benediction
of Pope Adrian the VII. He suffers untold hard-
ships, during a journey of seven or eight months,
which he regards as nothing in his joy at visiting
the Holy Places, and he resolves to spend the remain-
der of his life in visiting these sacred shrines, and
in labouring for the conversion of the heathen.
Meantime he receives extraordinary graces, and is
favoured with miraculous tokens.*

Or take the Life of St. Philip Neri, his contemporary. It is a great festival in Rome, on 11th
of February, 1590, when the bodies of the martyrs
SS. Papias and Maurus are being translated from
the Church of St. Martino de' Monti to that of Santa
Maria in Vallicella. Ten cardinals are in that
procession to meet the holy treasures, which are
consigned, by order of Pope Sixtus the V., to St.
Philip's custody. " Philip," says Bacci, his biographer,
" received them with such joy and exultation that he
could hardly contain himself. The usual flutterings of
his heart came on ; he leaped, and showed his intense
delight, by extraordinary motions of his whole body."†

---

* Life of St. Ignatius, Orat. Series, cap. x.
† Life of St. Philip Neri, Orat. Series, p. 153. Ed. 1849

Again : St. Camillus of Lellis is taken by Cardinal
Sfondrato to see the body of St. Cecilia, just then
discovered in Rome, before which he is rapt almost
in ecstacy. He visited the holy house at Loreto
many times, as well as the Sanctuary at Assisi, and
never went through Sienna without visiting the house
of St. Catherine; this, too, was his constant practice
wherever there were celebrated sanctuaries, or remarkable relics of saints.* .

Turning, at length, to the special subject under
consideration, it has been already noticed that,
among the relics with which the Church is stored,
those of our Lord and His Mother claim pre-eminence.† Every memento of the thirty-three years of
His life on earth demands the special veneration of
Christians. The places sanctified by His presence
(known as the " Holy Places")—Bethlehem, Nazareth,
Galilee, Jerusalem, Mount Thabor, the Garden of
Gethsemane, Calvary, the Mount of Olives,—all these,
and others, have ever had an awful attraction for
believers in the Incarnation, and for over eighteen
hundred years have formed the world's great point
of pilgrimage. So with even greater force has it
been with the relics which have been yet more
closely associated with His life on earth. His sacred

---

* Life of St. Camillus, Orat. Series, p. 384.
† The Congregation of Rites prohibits the commingling of such relics, with
other relics of saints.

garments, — the instruments of His Passion — the Cross—the nails—the spear—the crown of thorns— all bring vividly to mind the God made Man ; and all are filled to overflowing with the virtue which went out from Him.

In their accounts of the Passion of Jesus Christ, all the four evangelists make mention of our Lord's garments—more or less fully. All of them allude to the casting of lots, but St. John alone explains that it was for the seamless Tunic that the lots were cast, and that the remaining garments were divided.

" The soldiers, therefore, when they had crucified him, took his garments (and they made four parts, to every soldier a part)—and also his Coat. Now the Coat was without seam, woven from the top throughout. And they said, let us not cut it, but let us cast lots for it, whose it shall be."*

St. Matthew and St. John repeat the prophecy of the Psalmist : " They have parted my garments among them, and for my vesture they have cast lots."† Other passages in the Gospels name our Lord's Tunic as the *direct instrument* of numberless miracles, which are thus recorded:

" And when the men of that place had knowledge of him, they sent into all that country, and brought

---

* John xix. 23, 24.
† Ps. xxi. 19.

to him all that were diseased. And they besought
him that they might *touch the hem of his garment, and
as many as touched were made whole.*"*

" And all the multitude sought to touch him, for
virtue went out from him, and healed all.†

And running through that whole country, they began
to carry about in beds those that were sick, where they
heard he was.   And whithersoever he entered, into
towns or into villages or cities, they laid the sick in the
streets, and besought him that they might *touch the
hem of his garment : and as many as touched him were made
whole.*"‡

Looking to these passages from the Gospels, it
seems probable that the miracles wrought by the
agency of our Blessed Lord's garments far exceeded
in number all the other miracles which the evangelists
record during His three years' ministry.

The other passages refer to the miraculous cure
of the woman with· the issue of blood, recorded in
the first three Gospels :

" And behold a woman who was troubled with an
issue of blood, twelve years, came *behind him, and*

---

* Matt. xiv., 35, 36.
† Luke vi., 19.
‡ Mark vi. 55, 56.

touched the hem of his garment. For she said within herself, If I shall *touch only his garment I shall be healed.**

And Jesus said: *who is it that touched me ?* And all denying, Peter and they that were with him said: Master, the multitudes *throng and press thee,* and dost thou say, who touched me ? And Jesus said: *Some-body hath touched me, for I know that virtue has gone out from me.* And the woman, seeing that she was not hid, came trembling and fell down before his feet; and declared before all the people *for what cause she had touched him, and how she was immediately healed.* But he said to her: Daughter, thy faith hath made thee whole; go thy way in peace."†

What wonder then,—since the Gospels lay such stress upon the garments of our Lord, of which the Royal Psalmist had chaunted his prophecy some thousand years before,—that the Fathers of the Church recognized in them a deep mysterious meaning ? St. Cyprian : " The Coat of our Lord Jesus Christ is not divided, not cut up, but after the casting of the lot is given away, a whole, inviolate, undivided garment. He who causes a division in the Church cannot bear the Coat of Christ." St. Augustine : " What else does this Coat signify but love, that love which

---

* Matt. ix. 20.
† Luke viii. 45.

nobody shall divide? What else is it but unity?"

Tradition loves to tell how Mary wove that Sacred Tunic,* as Anna had done for the infant Samuel:— like the valiant woman in Scripture:

"She hath sought wool and flax, and hath wrought by the counsel of her hands"—"and her fingers have taken hold of the spindle."†

The revelations of St. Bridget and of Mary of Agreda speak of the work of Mary's hands. Other tradition tells how that Tunic—"fashioned with great art"—grew with our Lord's growth,‡—like the garments of the Israelites in the desert, of which the Scripture tells—"The raiment with which thou wast covered hath not decayed for age, and thy foot is not worn, lo, this is the fortieth year."§

Preachers and divines have dwelt upon the identification of the Holy Robe with the mysteries of our Lord's life; now in triumph, now in abjection; "One while, shining white as snow on Thabor at the Transfiguration; another, in the Garden, as on Calvary, drenched with tears, and holy sweat, and precious blood."‖

---

* St. Bonaventure, Suarez, Albertus Magnus.
† Prov. xxxi.
‡ Salermon: "Jesu crescente, ipsam etiam crevisse."
§ Deut. viii. 4.
‖ Abbé Bénard.

One further manifestation, say the legends of the Mosel valley, yet lies hid in the counsels of God; to be fulfilled, when, clad in this Robe, in full sight of every created soul, He shall come in glory to judge both the living and the dead.

CHAPTER III.

THE HOLY COAT OF TREVÈS: ITS HISTORY AND
AUTHENTICITY.

ENGLISH historians will be loth to concede to Trèves
the claim to be the birth-place of St. Helena; as
they are nearly unanimous that the Empress, as
well as her son Constantine, was born in Britain.
The claims of York have been strongly maintained,
but yet more weighty are those of Colchester. Helena
(according to the antiquarian Leland and others) was
daughter of King Coilus, or Côel, who first enclosed
that city within walls, and so beautified it that it
derived from him its name; and its inhabitants, in
memory of the discovery of the Cross by St. Helena,
have adopted as the city arms a knotty cross between
four crowns.

But, as her spiritual birthplace, the claim of
Trèves is open to no doubt at all: and she with
her son, who held their court there, embraced
Christianity about the time of the miraculous appari-
tion to Constantine of the luminous cross, with the
inscription, "In this conquer" (A.D. 311). Constan-

tine's victory over Maxentius, and conversion, immediately followed; and with his mother he received
baptism, probably at the hands of St. Agritius, the
then Bishop of Trèves (312).* Later on (in A.D. 325),
Constantine summoned the assembly of the Council
of Nicæa; and in the following year we find him
writing to St. Macarius, Bishop of Jerusalem, on
the subject of building a magnificent church on
Mount Calvary. Of this undertaking St. Helena
personally assumed the charge, and, although then
at the age of nearly four-score years, performed
the journey to Jerusalem, prompted, as the early
historians tell,† by a divine admonition to ascertain
the site of the Holy Sepulchre, and to discover the
instruments of our Lord's Passion.

Besides devoting most of her immense fortune,
and her imperial palace to the service of God, the
Empress further enriched the Church of Trèves with
the gift of a chest of precious relics, collected in
the Holy Land and elsewhere, which, through the
hands, and with the sanction of Pope Sylvester,
she consigned to her chosen city. These are believed
to have included—in addition to the seamless Robe—
other such important relics as a nail of the true
Cross, several portions of the Cross itself, the body

---

* At this time the Empress Helena would have attained her sixty-fifth year.
† Eusebius, Socrates, Rufinus, St. Paulinus, &c.

of St. Matthias, and the head of St. Cornelius, Pope and martyr. Hence Pope Leo the X., in his Bull of 1515, comes to speak in such terms as these of the Church of Trèves: "on account of its venerable antiquity, and its foundation by the Prince of the Apostles, of the treasures of its relics, and of its princely endowments by Constantine and other Emperors, has attained such renown as to have earned the title of the second Rome, the mistress of the provinces, and the first of the Churches of Germany and Gaul." The same Pope goes on to allude to its ever constant adherence to the Catholic faith and the See of Rome through long centuries of strife and trouble.

As the frontier city it had ever borne the brunt of the ceaseless wars, pillage, and rapine extending from the fifth to the ninth Century. Upon it had burst the furious irruptions of Attila and the Huns, of Norsemen and Vandals, who found ample means of satisfying their greed in the wealth within its walls. Marvellous it is, then, that in such stormy times, the guardians of its sacred treasures—with all their zeal and devotion—should have been able to preserve the heritage entrusted them. Hidden away, and buried in unknown resting places, the relics were preserved from pillage and destruction when all else was in jeopardy. Few would know the secret, and these might in many instances fall victims to their foes, or die with their secret undivulged, rather than confide their trust imprudently. Archives would be ransacked, scattered, lost, or burnt; if indeed their preservation—had it been possible—might not have proved still more dangerous to the safe keeping of the Church's treasures. Hence from these and whatever other causes, the fact remains that for centuries together no documentary evidence can be traced in regard to the Relic of the Holy Coat. The exact dates of the twenty-four bishops who occupied the See of Trèves between St. Maternus (A.D. 120) and St. Agritius (312) cannot be accurately determined. The same holds good, of course, in the case of all relics of extreme antiquity throughout the Christian world, depending as they do on but scanty documentary proof, and that little but very rarely contemporaneous. But the documents, though not contemporaneous, bear witness to the unwritten belief of earlier times, and this again in its turn testifies to the pre-existence of the subject matter to which it relates.

In the case of the Holy Coat. Before its connection with Trèves, we are confronted with a silence of well nigh 300 years, from the Crucifixion to St. Helena's journey to Jerusalem. Then St. Helena would not have found it with the instruments of the Passion (which it was customary to bury near the victims), for it was the property of the Roman soldier who had won it by cast of the dice. He would look to retaining it for use, or to disposing of it at such a price as the excellence of its fabric might warrant. The garments of malefactors were considered the perquisite of the executioners (is it not so to the present day?); and the early Church writers consider that the intrinsic excellence of the seamless Tunic alone (humanly) deterred them from dividing it. Intact, it was of precious value; severed in pieces, it would be worthless.

There is a striking passage by the late Fr. Faber, to whom all English-speaking Catholics, here and at the Antipodes, owe a debt of gratitude for his many deep and heart-stirring thoughts upon the objects of the Faith. He is writing on the first of the three hours of the Crucifixion, and of Mary's part beneath the Cross. He says: "Near the Cross they are dicing for His garments. . . . She saw those garments, those relics which were beyond all price the world could give, in the hands of miserable sinners who would sacrilegiously clothe themselves therewith. . . . Now sinners were to wear them, and to carry them into unknown haunts of drunkenness and sin. Yet what was it but a type? The whole of an unclean world was to clothe itself in the beautiful justice of her Son. As Jacob had been blessed in Esau's garments, so should all mankind be blessed in the garments of their elder Brother.

"Then there was the seamless Tunic which she herself had wrought for Him. The unity of His Church was figured there. She saw them cast lots for it. She saw to whom it had fallen. One of her first loving duties to the Church will be to recover it for the faithful as a relic."*

Then, again, would not our Lord's friends be anxious to recover every memorial of Him? Probably amongst His followers there must have been many persons of wealth, of influence, and position. Scripture certainly names two such who were His disciples "secretly" and "for fear of the Jews," Nicodemus, and the rich man, Joseph of Arimathæa, and the influence of the latter was sufficient to gain the Body of Jesus from Pilate. The centurion, too, who at the last confessed His Divinity, might perhaps be added to these. Is it, then, unreasonable to ask: Would such as these, with their faith and knowledge, and with the recollection of that Friday afternoon ever present to their minds—would they be likely to spare any effort, any risk or expense to recover and preserve every least relic of Him?

---

* Faber, "Foot of the Cross," p. 293 (Ed. 1858). Great writers have remarked that the principal relics of our Lord were only permitted to appear at the epoch when the Church had acquired her liberty, and could allow of their public veneration.

With all possible allowance for their timidity and fear at such a time,—in recollection of．the earthquake, the darkness, the portends that had appeared in the city of Jerusalem, of which men went whispering in horror and perplexity—admitting all this, we know that within three short days their hearts were re-assured, and that, a few weeks later, when the day of Pentecost had come, the most timid were changed to heroes whom nothing could daunt : when the new-born Church went forth upon its Mission, un-deterred by fear of men. It seems, then, impossible that they should have shrunk from doing what thousands of believers at the present day would hope they might themselves have had the grace and strength to do, namely, to run any risk in order to save these precious relics ; and, when secured, to hand them down to their successors (secretly, doubtless, for fear of damage and sacrilege) as a precious heirloom. Then what more probable, after Constantine's victories and conversion, when the Church was at length established in peace and liberty, than that these precious relics should have been handed over to the Empress, St. Helena,—whose errand would be gladly hailed by them,—to be pre-served in perpetuity for Christ's Church ? This is mere conjecture, of course ; but since the facts have not been told us, it is at least more reasonable,

as well as reverend, than to suppose that the infant
Church should have left unheeded the memorials of
its Divine Founder. Thus, then, St. Helena, having
been divinely prompted to undertake her mission,
may reasonably be believed to have been led on to
the discovery of this sacred Relic, once already
providentially spared from destruction.

Presupposing, now, the actual arrival of the Holy
Tunic at Trèves, by the gift of the Empress in 326
or 327 (she is recorded to have died in the month
of August, 328), we are again confronted—as far
as documentary evidence is concerned—with another
eclipse of the relic for five long centuries. Evidence
enough exists of the unbroken line of archbishops
and bishops ruling the See of Trèves from that
date, the time of St. Agritius, through the fifteen
hundred years and more, which bring us down to
its present occupant, Bishop Korum. And this is
much to the point when we enter upon the troublesome times from the fifth to the ninth Century, to
which allusion has been made; though even this
evidence comes to us, not from indigenous sources,
but from the incidental mention of foreign writers.
We have already briefly noted the importance of
Trèves in the third and fourth Centuries, and how
it had then become a great centre of civilization.
Eminent archbishops and bishops — such as St.

Maximinus, St. Felix, St. Paulinus, and others—
had ruled the See, men of great erudition and com-
manding position, who took prominent part in the
great questions of the day. Then we enter upon
the era of the great Princes ot the Church—of
European fame—who ruled at Trèves. Within its
walls stately churches had risen: no less than four
great Benedictine abbeys were its seats of learning;
yet from all these founts of knowledge, human and
divine, scarcely a record of the early past has been
derived. Literature, works of science and art,
historical records, family archives,—all, or nearly
all, have been effaced. Monasteries and libraries
were ravaged again and again, till, at the descent
of the Normans in 882, a universal pillage, lasting
four entire days, ended in a conflagration which
obliterated all but the merest vestiges of the Trèves
of old. Deep down beneath the modern town may
be found the traces of the ruthless waves of destruction which swept over the suffering city. Canon
Wilmowski, a well-known archæologist, has pointed
out—the result of recent excavations,—three distinct
strata of ashes and cinder at varying depths,
which mark consecutive paths of the destroyers.
Hence it is but simple truth to say that Trèves
possesses no record of its glories in the third and
fourth Centuries from the pens of its own historians.

All have to be gleaned from foreign sources. Can we then wonder that no written record should remain of its hidden relics, buried out of sight for all those years in their silent chambers? On this reflection, Dr. Willems (to whose powerful work I am much indebted), remarks, in some such words as these: " If, however, we have to mourn the loss of many wished-for documents relating to our Relic, *one* at least is left to us,—one archive which no tempests could destroy, no scourge efface:—the love and veneration which the memory of their treasure has always kindled in the hearts of the Faithful: which will keep it ever burning there, when archives shall have gone to dust, and graven stone and brass have perished."

1. The Gesta Trevirorum.

It is true that a brief reference to the gift of relics by St. Helena is found in the writings of the monk Almann in the ninth Century: but with this exception, the earliest remaining records of the Holy Coat are found in the " Annals of Trèves," the " Gesta. Treviorum."

With the close of the stormy centuries referred to above, the Benedictines of the great Monastery of St. Matthias could at length find liberty and leisure for peaceful study ; and from the time of the.

departure of the invader they commenced the work of re-collecting from all parts the materials for their labour. All countries were laid under contribution to their needs, and they applied themselves with zeal and patient industry to repair their losses. Then it was that they commenced their careful chronicle, gathering together as far as possible, the threads of their country's history, and recording day by day—so to speak—the narrative of current events. It is in their record, then, that we read of the construction of the eastern choir of the Cathedral by Archbishop Hillin, and of the consecration of the high altar by Archbishop John in 1196.

Some portions of these annals must have been written at a later date than the events they record, yet well within the memory of persons then living. The discovery of the body of St. Matthias the Apostle, by Archbishop Bruno, is here related, and its deposition beside the body of St. Eucharius. They further testify to the existence of the Holy Coat, with the nail and other relics, in the Cathedral of St. Peter.

2. THE LETTER OF BARBAROSSA.

The much contested letter from the Emperor Barbarossa to Archbishop Hillin would, if perfectly established, form a testimony of a few years earlier.

The Emperor had fallen under the displeasure of Pope Adrian the IV. (the English Pope), and seeking to shake the Archbishop's allegiance, wrote him an eulogistic letter, in which he lays strong stress on his dignity as " Primate this side the Alps," and as *custodian of the mystical Tunic of Christ.**** But whatever may be decided as to the authenticity of the letter, it is certainly quoted in MSS. of the twelfth Century, and is therefore not wholly value-less as indicating the belief of the times immediately preceding.

A later datum is found in an account by the Benedictine Lambert of Liege, about the year 1186, of the discovery of the body of St. Matthias, before mentioned, in which he alludes to the relics given by St. Helena, through the hands of Pope Sylvester, to the custody of St. Agritius ; especially naming among them the seamless Tunic.

3. THE DIPLOMA OF ST. SYLVESTER.

Another document—reproduced in the Gesta Tre-virorum about the year 1100, and quoted by every writer upon this subject—is described as the " Diploma of St. Sylvester" (314 to 335), in which the Pope confers, or rather renews and confirms, the Primacy

* This letter, it should be observed, was written forty-years before the redis-covery of the Tunic in the Cathedral at Trèves.

of the Church of Trèves over Gauls and Germans,
in the person of St. Agritius of Antioch. This is
not generally looked upon as an original document.
It is considered to be drawn in no authentic or
customary form; the original is believed to have
been lost, and the text, as it stands, to have been
recast in its present form by Bishop Volusianus in
the fifth Century. Writers of weight, whose historic
criticism is held in great repute—Hontheim and
the Bollandist Papebroch—recognized it as "historic
testimony of the *fifth Century.*" They affirm that its
details are historically true; and that, although it
be not the original text of St. Sylvester, the "essence
is preserved." Also, that Bishop Volusianus has
neither garbled nor falsified, but that in the form in
which his transcript appears, it fills in great measure
the place of the missing text.

4. The Life of St. Agritius.

All writers upon the subject of the Holy Coat
attach much importance to the work of an unknown
author of the eleventh Century—"The Life of St.
Agritius"; mainly, perhaps, on account of the care
and accuracy with which he chronicles contemporary
events, and so affords at least a trustworthy record
of the traditions of his own time. If less confidence
is attached to his record of events which occurred

in the fourth Century, it is because one or two well-known and important facts of that era have passed unnoticed in his pages. It will be enough to instance the prominent part taken by St. Agritius at the Council of Arles in 314, of which he makes no mention.

As to the date of this work there seems no positive certainty; Professor Waitz places it between 1050 and 1072; Schmitt connects it with the first half of the eleventh Century, but not earlier than 1019. Its author is very distinct in asserting that St. Agritius was charged by Pope Sylvester to *convey* the Relic to Trèves: a statement which seems to illustrate, and to be confirmed by the incident depicted on the " ivory tablet," to which reference will be made presently. He is also earnest in protesting against too ready credence being given to mere popular rumours and tales; while he lays much stress on the value of a constant tradition, derived from trustworthy ancestors.

At least the testimony of the author of the " Life of St. Agritius" is a respectable guarantee of the belief—that had come down to him and his contemporaries—that in the Treasury of the Cathedral ("in sui thesauri gazophylatio") there was preserved a Relic which they acknowledged and revered as the seamless Tunic of our Lord.

Such a biography, it should also be remembered, would not be aimed at 'the illiterate and the vulgar: before the age of printing there would be no inducement to appeal to popularity: the work would only find its way to the desks of the learned, who would be judges of the subject; or would be read aloud in the Congregations of Religious.

5. THE IVORY TABLET.

From the earliest times until the period of the Revolution, there had been preserved in the Cathedral Treasury at Trèves a tablet of ivory, representing, in elabòrate bas-relief, an incident which is believed to be closely connected with the story of the Holy Coat. During the troubles of the Revolution, this tablet appears to have been unaccountably lost, and it was only re-discovered at Antwerp in 1836. Prior to this date, it is traced to a private collection, in which (as also in the auction rooms at Antwerp) it was described as representing " the reception of a solemn procession with relics at Trèves by the Empress Helena." How this work of art came to be lost remains unexplained. The relics and other treasures of the churches of Trèves had been carefully removed to places of safety afar off, and it can only be inferred that the tablet was lost sight of by inadvertence.

The ivory tablet has well deserved the consideration it has received from archæologists and critics. It comes as an independent testimony, from a wholly unexpected quarter, to supply a void in the scanty documentary evidence, and further serves to illustrate, while it is itself elucidated by, the text of the "Diploma of St. Sylvester." But to describe it :— Upon an oblong plate of ivory, measuring about $10\frac{1}{4}$ inches in length by $5\frac{1}{2}$ inches in height, is carved in bas-relief a procession of men advancing towards a Christian temple (consisting of nave, aisles, and transept). At the entrance of the temple is seated a female figure, in the jewelled robes and diadem of an empress, bearing on her shoulder a cross of great size, who with extended hand, appears to be welcoming the arrival of the procession. On the left of the tablet the procession terminates with a car drawn by two horses of the heroic Roman type; and upon the car are seated two high dignitaries of the Church, in pontifical vestments and wearing the Pallium,* who carry on their knees a sumptuous reliquary. The side of the car is adorned with a bas-relief in panel, representing three other figures in habit of bishops.

The back-ground is almost entirely occupied by a massive building of apparently three stories, with

---

* The Pallium was ordinarily bestowed only on patriarchs, primates, arch bishops, or metropolitans.

arches, columns, and cornice (much in the style and proportions of the Porta Nigra at Trèves, which indeed it strikingly suggests); and in all the windows of the building are seen figures, with thuribles or censers in their hands. To the extreme left of this great structure, and as if adjoining it, a portion of another Christian church would seem to be intended, as though the procession were starting from that point; and at its summit,—framed within an arch,— is shown the sculptured half-figure of our Saviour, with nimbus enclosing the Cross.

The description here attempted needs indeed a reference to the fac-simile which accompanies this chapter; and, although the reproduction is much reduced in size from the actual carving, it may serve to assist the reader in following the narrative it is believed to illustrate.

It will probably be inferred already, that the scene depicted here is intended to pourtray the solemn transfer of the relics presented by St. Helena to Trèves; but it may be necessary to point out its fitness and congruity in detail. Witness the Cathedral to the right of the picture; the figure of the Empress at its doors, her personality indicated by the massive cross she bears, and with which her name was ever to be associated. The two bishops (of highest possible rank, as the Pallium denotes) seated upon the car, represent, as they readily suggest, the twin saints first connected with the history of the Relic—SS. Sylvester and Agritius. The carved figures on the car find fitting antitypes in Trèves first bishops,— those three, who at St. Peter's bidding brought the Faith to the valley of the Mosel,—SS. Eucharius, Valerius, and Maternus. The Head of our Saviour, too, thus prominently placed, is taken to indicate that those relics are His: and various writers have also supposed, that the temple from which the procession would appear to be issuing, is intended for the Basilica of "the Saviour"—the great Lateran Church at Rome —the Mother Church of Christendom.

Now for what purpose was the ivory tablet intended? At the Exposition of the Holy Tunic in 1512, under Archbishop Richard (von Gréffenklau), it is related by Bishop Enen, his coadjutor, and an eye witness, that upon the opening of the relic chamber there was disclosed, in addition to many other relics, an important reliquary of wood and precious ivory, sealed with a seal, and bearing the inscription, " This is the seamless Tunic of our Lord and Saviour, Jesus Christ." Later examination of the tablet shows it to be bevelled or mitred along its edges, and evidently thus fashioned with a view to its insertion as a panel in some sort of frame-work. This tallies with Bishop Enen's account, although no trace remains of the rest of the reliquary which it adorned.

As regards the date at which the ivory bas-relief is supposed to have been produced—The archæologists of Frankfort in 1846 assigned it to the fourth Century: Kraus and others prefer to attribute it to the fifth or sixth Centuries: and one or two others as late as the ninth; but the great majority of critics determine it as belonging to the fifth or, at latest, the sixth Century. Thus the testimony of the ivory tablet comes with great force as a proof of the consignment of the Holy Coat to Trèves by St. Helena; and its witness is strengthened by its supposed connection with the Diploma of St. Sylvester.

THE PEOPLE'S LEGENDS.

In the face of the warning issued by the writer of the Life of St. Agritius, some brief reference may be permitted to the legends interpenetrating the entire valley of the Mosel, and spreading far beyond it, having for their burthen the deposition and the sojourn of the Holy Tunic at Trèves; and if any justification for such reference is needed, it is to be found in the fact that, (1) with whatever admixture of myth or fable such legends are commonly presented, there always exists a foundation of truth, however embellished or disfigured; and (2) that legends are valuable, if only from their great antiquity, which often dates back to periods unreached by any records of reliable history. The "Holy Grail," "King Arthur," and "Siegfried" are instances which will be recognized; and in the present case writers have numbered no less than nine or ten distinct legends, having reference to the Holy Coat at Trèves.

Of these, perhaps, the best known is the "Song of Orendel"; of which it may be said that, with whatever extravagance and triviality it may be surrounded, yet its direct subject matter is the translation of the Sacred Relic to Trèves, and its preservation there till the end of time, when, "seated on His throne, and clad in this robe, God will come to judge the world."

CHAPTER IV.

The Garments of Our Lord.

We now come to the general appearance of the Holy Coat, as it is seen behind the huge covering of plate glass, which forms the front of the reliquary in which it is exposed. Within this reliquary the Tunic is suspended by a rod passing through the sleeves. It measures about five feet in length, from the neck opening (from which the sleeves spring in continuous line) to the bottom fringe of the garment. The skirt is about three feet six inches in width, and the sleeves one foot in depth. Its colour may be described as a brown of medium intensity, inclining to a shade of dark fawn. The appearance of the fabric hardly affords opportunity for a guess at its actual material. It suggests to the sight the possibilities of such diverse materials as silk, fine wool, or very soft cotton, while at the same time it has something of the "frizzy" appearance associated with crape.

The entire Tunic, both back and front, (with its protecting coverings), consists of three layers of material, differing in the front from those at the back of the garment. The front has been at one time covered with a rich and sumptuous material of oriental damask, figured in geometric patterns of lozenged squares in gold and purple, enclosing representations of birds in pairs. Of this front covering only shreds of remnants are left ; indeed the greater part had already disappeared in 1810, as is related by Cordel, the then Vicar-General. This covering formerly concealed the actual Tunic ; owing, however, to the gradual decay of the protecting material, the object which now meets the eye is none other than the veritable garment itself.

The back of the garment is protected, as *was* the front, by a covering, though of a different material, —a sort of web or gauze of considerable strength, and woven so widely that the texture of the Tunic beneath can plainly be seen between the threads.

Within : the entire tunic, back as well as front, is lined with a light brown silk of great substance, forming a complete inner coat of similar size and shape to the actual relic, to which it is everywhere attached. The inner lining is composed of numerous pieces of silk sewn together, many of which have borders of variously coloured stripes ; the pieces being so attached that the stripes run irregularly and follow no precise pattern.

To the strength and consistency of this lining is greatly due the preservation of the Holy Coat, and its promise of security for the future. Nothing is known of the actual date of this silk lining, nor of the material of web or gauze which protects the back of the garment: but both are of much later date than the fragmentary remains of the broidered damask, which can only be classified with the most ancient oriental liturgical vestments, and are variously assigned by learned connoisseurs to the sixth, the fifth, and even the fourth Century. Dr. Bock,—renowned for his experience and judgment of oriental fabrics, and those of the early Christian era,—unhesitatingly ascribes the damask to the early part of the sixth Century, and during the reign of Justinian. This would correspond with the actual time of the restoration of the Cathedral, under the great Archbishop Nicetius (A.D. 527-566)—whose praises have been sung by St. Gregory of Tours—who might on such an occasion reasonably be expected to review and re-arrange the treasures of his church, and provide for their seemly and reverend keeping.

To this time, too—as we have already seen—some authors ascribe the "chasse" of wood and figured ivory, discovered by Bishop Enen at the solemn Exposition of 1512. It would seem, then, that even so early as the date of the broidered damask,—

carefully as the Relic would have been tended,—
this covering was deemed necessary for its preser·
vation ; and thereby the fabric of the Holy Coat
itself is shown to pertain to a far higher antiquity,
and easily to the apostolic age.

As to the actual material of the Holy Coat, nothing
decisive has been ascertained. At the Exposition
of 1512, experts were unable to agree whether it was
of silk, wool, flax, or fine cotton, or of some combina·
tion of two or more of these. Bishop Enen, who at
that time—as he tells us—"frequently held it in his
hands," describes the feeling of it to the touch as
"something quite peculiar,—neither so soft as velvet,
nor so rough as serge." Another witness on the same
occasion, considered it to be a very fine description
of linen. In 1844, it was believed by an expert—a
cloth manufacturer, who examined it by the aid of
lenses—to be composed of fine wool ; while at the
same time the Vicar-General Cordel describes the
fineness and delicacy of its threads as resembling
muslin. The searching scrutiny of 1890, testing it
by touch, and by its aspect under the microscope,
went but little further than to demonstrate the marked
distinction between the Relic itself, and the remnants
of the silken covering which formerly protected it ;
although these were in fact so closely amalgamated
as to be indistinguishable to the naked eye. Hence

the mystery surrounding the very material of the
Holy Coat, becomes a strong testimony to its genuine-
ness : and the fact that the material corresponds
with no known fabric which has come down to us,
points at least to a very remote antiquity. If this
is but a negative testimony, it certainly has weight
in assigning the Relic itself to a period far more
ancient than its protective coverings.

Before entering upon the question of the numerous
existing relics of our Lord's garments, it may be
useful to make some little inquiry into the customary
clothing of the Jewish people at the time of His
sojourn on earth, and into the nature and variety of
the garments He may Himself be presumed to have
worn. Here the subject is by no means clear, and
evidence is difficult to obtain. In spite of the pro-
verbial invariability of oriental habits and customs
(like the laws of Medes and Persians), we can hardly
trust the description of the Jews in the Old Testament
history to represent faithfully the actual state of
things so many centuries later, as the time of our
Lord's manhood and Crucifixion. The Gospels give
no indication of our Saviour's attire : in their history
the outward man disappears in the illumination of
His divine acts; and the only details to be found
in Scripture, relating to the ceremonial vestments
of priests, can be no great criterion of the manner
of the garments worn by the multitudes.

It is agreed, though, by most writers on the subject, that the ordinary dress among the higher and middle-class Jews comprised at least three distinct articles: (1) an under garment or garments worn next the body, and of the nature of a long shirt (*interula*, *subucula*); (2) the tunic (*tunica*); and (3) the mantle or cloak (*toga*, *pallium*). The tunic would be of different lengths, shorter, both in body and sleeves, for the labouring class, whom it would otherwise impede; but for persons of class and wealth it would be fuller, more ornate, and in length reaching to the feet. So, too, the superior working classes might adopt a longer tunic for ceremonial or holiday occasions.

The mantle would be in one piece, oval or rectangular, with merely an aperture through which to pass the head; and it would fall in folds to about the knees. The material and colour, too, might be expected to alter with the class and condition of the wearer: linen, cotton, wool, and the hair of animals—camels and goats; all were placed under contribution, and the colours would vary equally, from the undyed material to the tints most in vogue. The pure white were adopted for feasts and ceremonies; while for different occasions, purple and other colours, plain or embroidered, simple or ornate, were sought for by the higher classes.

In considering the actual garments which our Lord may be presumed to have worn, it is needful to remember the distinct and varied phases of His life, to which a different form of attire would seem. but fitting. He passed through infancy, youth, manhood: the humble obscurity of the house of Nazareth, and His labour in the workshop of St. Joseph,—these are in complete contrast with the life of His three years' ministry, when all men called Him "Rabbi." In the first case, as Dr. Willems points out, he would probably be habited in the shorter tunic and sleeves of the working class; in His public life we might expect to find Him in the garments suited to His altered condition of life. In the contrast He Himself deigns to draw between St. John's coming and His own, He refers to the austerity of the Baptist on the one side, and on the other He describes Himself as having come " eating and drinking." Now such a contrast may not unreasonably be supposed to extend to His general manner of life, apparel included. He has not told us how He was clad; but of the Baptist, His evangelist has distinctly written that he " was clothed with camel's hair, and a leathern girdle about his loins."* Our Lord pursues the same

---

* St. Mark, i. 6.

contrast between His own disciples, and those of
the Holy Baptist.*

Then, again, He is in contact with all classes: with
the high-born and the great, as well as the poor
and obscure; and that, too, from the standpoint
of their Law-giver and Teacher. The rich young
man addresses Him as "Good Master." It would
seem, then, incongruous to depict Him during the
three years of his ministry, as clad in the meaner
garments of the extreme poor. Poor He was indeed:
but the devout women who followed Him were, at
least some of them, of presumable means and position,
and would naturally minister to His necessities. The
box of precious ointment would be but a type of
the generosity and devotion with which they would
contribute to His personal needs. Thus, then, it
would happen that at the time of His death there
must have been numerous articles of raiment existing,
which had been sanctified by the contact of His
Sacred Body; and which were destined, hereafter,
to be brought forward into the light of day, to become
the objects of the loving veneration of those who
should believe in Him.

These few remarks may serve to account for
the many probably existing relics of our Lord's
raiment. But in pursuing this further subject, it is

---

* Id. lll. 18, 19.

requisite also to bear in mind the many titles under which different portions of His clothing are described. Thus we find the terms mantle, coat, vesture, tunic, the purple garment,* the white garment,—† all of which find specific mention in Scripture. Neither must we forget that the actual clothing, of which He was stripped on Calvary, is described by all four evangelists, and by Old Testament prophecy,‡ *in the plural* (*vestimenta*). And these, moreover, are expressly named, both by the psalmist and St. John,§ *exclusive of* the " seamless robe," for which the lots were cast.

It need, then, be no matter for surprise, if the relics of His sacred garments—treasured up and down His Church—should prove to be very numerous. The part, too, might be frequently attributed to the whole ; and, as we have already seen, portions of material which had been applied as protective covering to actual relics, and in time become scarcely distinguishable therefrom—which had grown old in their protective service, till themselves required renewal— would not unnaturally be deemed to have themselves acquired a title to veneration : not to be cast aside, nor treated with less respect than those handkerchiefs and napkins which had touched the

---

* St. John, xix. 2.
† St. Luke, xxlii. 2.
‡ Ps. xxi. 19.
§ St. John, xlx. 24.

body of St. Paul, and by that touch acquired
mysterious virtue.* Wholly apart, then, from any
hypotheses of miraculous increase, like the widow's
oil and meal, or such as that referred to by St.
Cyril of Jerusalem, who tells how—but twenty-five
years after the discovery of the Holy Cross—portions
of the sacred wood were already spread throughout
the world (which he compares with the miraculous
feeding of the five thousand in the Gospel);—or by
St. Paulinus, who relates that though its fragments
were daily detached to satisfy the devotion of the
Faithful, yet the Holy Tree suffered no diminution—
Setting aside such hypotheses as unnecessary for the
present purpose, no difficulty need be occasioned
to the Christian mind by the variety of relics of the
garments of our Lord, which come with good authority,
and with the venerable tradition of the Churches.

No need here to give in detail the instances which
are forthcoming. Learned authors have been at
pains to classify and record the more notable relics
with which the Church is stored; but some notice
is required of the alleged cases in which rival claims
to the possession of identical relics have been sustained.
Nor are such statements surprising. Consider for
a moment the various accounts of the recent Exposition of the great Relic at Trèves,—the multitudinous

---

* Acts, xix. 12.

comments poured forth in the journals of all Europe. Some writers, doubtless, would be in a position to be well-informed ; but with the great majority, what distortion of facts, what hopeless muddle of inference ! A certain event had to be chronicled and accounted for ; and too often the wildest surmises, the fragments of idle legends, the sneers of the avowedly irreligious, the smart criticisms of free-thought and infidelity,— these have formed tho basis of the information vouch-safed to a curious and credulous public. How many scores of writers have discussed with facile pen the story of the Holy Coat ? The teaching of the Church —Councils—Fathers—Papal Infallibility, and what not :—all have been dragged in, and nothing has come amiss to the hands of certain scribes, whose Gospel a Catholio child, with its Catechism, might easily disprove.

One objection in particular has been cited in the English press, as fatal to the authenticity of the Holy Coat at Trèves: it is a sample of others, and may here be briefly traced.

The Tunic at Argenteuil.

To an article in a French journal—*La Liberté*— the British public is probably indebted for information which has been widely distributed through the English press, and which has been supposed to annihilate

the claim of Trèves to the ownership of the Holy
Tunic. The real Tunic, said the *Liberté*, was at
Argenteuil, near Paris :—there were undoubted proofs
of its authenticity :—it had been an object of devotion
for at least ten Centuries; and a Sovereign Pontiff,
Pope Gregory the XVI., had sanctioned the veneration
shown to it.

Here was a plain categorical statement, which
might have afforded ample scope for controversy;
but that its main facts had never been disputed :—
save one, viz., that it was, or claimed to be, the
" seamless Tunic" of our Lord—the " Tunica inconsutilis" of St. John's Gospel.

The church at Argenteuil certainly possesses a
revered relic of our Lord's clothing, of which St.
Gregory of Tours is the first historian. It is believed
to have been presented to the Monastery of Argenteuil
by Charlemagne, whose sister was abbess there.
Hidden away during times of trouble, it was redis-
covered in 1156. During the Revolution it was
torn in pieces, though subsequently recovered, and
the fragments, or most of them, again united. After
the Concordat, at the instance of the Bishop of
Versailles, Pope Pius the VII. authorized its being
restored to the veneration of the Faithful, and attached
to it a privileged altar.

But all this had ever been admitted; nor does

E

it appear, outside the newspapers, that any rivalry existed between Trèves and Argenteuil, regarding the undoubted relics which each of them possessed. Of the original form of the relic at Argenteuil it is impossible to speak with absolute certainty, owing to the injuries it sustained; but it is shown to have been of a totally different character to the Tunic of Trèves, than which it is *much smaller*, and of wholly *different material*—a kind of woven camel's hair, still found in the East. Its colour, too, is very much darker than the Trèves Tunic; and, unlike that, it has no sort of protective covering or lining. It is believed by those who are its natural custodians, and who must therefore be the most jealous of its good report, that it was an under-garment, and intended to be worn beneath the more ample Robe preserved at Trèves.

So much, then, for the rivalry which has been so much spoken of. It received its final quietus under singular and unexpected circumstances, even in *the presence of the Holy Coat at Trèves*. Some days before the solemn Exposition commenced, the Bishop of Trèves received a kind and friendly letter from the Bishop of Versailles, begging to be allowed to send three priests from Argenteuil, who might inspect the Holy Coat, with a view to comparing it with their own relic. To this proposal Mgr. Korum gladly acceded, and the priests arrived in Trèves three days before the solemn Exposition. Every facility was afforded them for a thorough scrutiny of the Relic, which was spread before them on a silken covering, in the Treasury of the Cathedral. Here they were enabled, by microscopic aid, to institute closest comparison of the texture of the Robe with that of Argenteuil, of which they had brought a portion, duly sealed and authenticated. The examination convinced them that the two relics were different garmen⁺s of our Lord: they stated in the most emphatic manner that they had never doubted the authenticity of the seamless Tunic,* and that their veneration towards it had been greatly increased by their visit, and by the close examination which had been graciously permitted them. They were, finally, able to assure the Bishop of Trèves of the falsity of the rumours which had got abroad ; which they had no difficulty in tracing to the garbled statement of a correspondent to the journals, who had misrepresented, whether accidentally or by design, an interview with one of their clergy.

---

* Before starting for Trèves, the parish priest of Argenteuil had informed his congregation from the pulpit that he was going to venerate the Holy Coat at Trèves.

CHAPTER V.

FORMER EXPOSITIONS OF THE HOLY COAT: AND ITS
WANDERINGS.

THE Cathedral Church (Domkirche) of St. Peter at
Trèves—the home of the Holy Coat—has undergone
many changes, since first the palace of old Roman
days gave place to the Christian temple : and, as
would be expected, the records of its early growth
and progress are no more than the history of the
various restorations, necessitated by the havoc of the
invader. Thus it came to be wholly renovated by
the Archbishop St. Nicetius (527-566), after partial
destruction by the Franks ; and thus again the work
of restoration was resumed by Archbishop Poppo
(1016-1047), after the ruin and disaster caused by
the Norman invaders.

With the advent of more peaceful times, the outward manifestation of the Christian Empire comes
into greater prominence. In the year 1050 we have
a Sovereign Pontiff, St. Leo the IX.,* visiting the

---

* St. Leo the IX. had been Bishop of Toul, and ruled that See (as Bishop
Bruno) for twenty-two years. During his Pontificate he twice visited Germany,
and he held a Council at Rheims.

Cathedral Church of St. Peter, Tréves.

city of Trèves; and in the year 1147 another Pope,
Eugenius the III., is welcomed within its walls. Half-
a-century later, Archbishop John, while completing
the restoration (in great 'measure the rebuilding)
commenced by his predecessors, spared no pains in
excavating to the very foundations of the building, in
order to discover the relics, to the existence of
which tradition had testified through centuries of
trouble. At length a large chest was discovered
embedded in masonry in the western choir, beneath
an altar of St. Nicholas. (This would be between
the two western towers, and underneath the spot
on which the organ now stands.)

The solemn translation of the Holy Coat took
place on the feast of SS. Philip and James, 1st May,
1196, when it was consigned to a shrine beneath
the high altar in the eastern choir. Here for more
than three centuries it remained undisturbed; nor is
there any record of its having been exposed for
veneration. Yet for all this, its recollection seems
never to have faded from the minds of men, in those
districts watered by the Mosel and the Rhine. They
were conscious of the possession of a priceless
treasure. As He who wore that Robe draws all
men to Himself, so, in its measure, did that sacred
Relic. They believed in it, and they loved it for
His sake.

•

EXPOSITION OF 1512.

Probably no such distinguished gathering had been seen in Trèves — at least since the visits of the Sovereign Pontiffs, above related, — as when the Emperor Maximilian convoked the Diet of the Empire in that city in 1512.

Surrounded by an immense retinue of princes of the Empire, of archbishops and bishops, mitred abbots, dukes and nobles,—accompanied by the Pope's legate, Cardinal Campeggio, and by the representatives of the Kings of France, Navarre, and England,— the sojourn of the Emperor at Trèves must indeed have transformed the face of the old-world city. Nor among this brilliant company of the high-born and the distinguished was the humble treasure of Trèves less appreciated, than by the simple peasants of the surrounding vine-clad hills. To the surprise, and, it would seem, to the no small perplexity of the Archbishop (the Prince Elector Richard von Greiffenklau), the Emperor expressed his formal desire to be shown the Sacred Tunic. Doubtless the Archbishop had good cause for embarrassment. In early times the only opportunities afforded for open and public displays of the veneration of relics were upon the occasions either of their discovery, or of their solemn translation to the temples in which they were

permanently to remain.* It might well seem doubtful,
then, if even the imperial "fiat" formed an adequate
reason for an innovation, for which no precedent
could be found in the actions of the long line of the
rulers of the See of St. Eucharius. The solemn
consignment of the Holy Coat to the high altar by
Archbishop John, in 1196, had for its object the rescue
of the Relic from its buried crypt, and its instalment
in a more fitting place of honour; but it was in
no sense a concession to private devotion. Then, too,
there was a well-remembered tradition of a former
attempt to un-house the holy Relic; which told how
the first to gaze within the coffer had been struck
with blindness. It is scarcely surprising, then,—as
Bishop Enen relates,—that the Archbishop acceded
with no little reluctance to the Emperor's wish. His
first act was to call for prayers in all the monasteries
and churches of the diocese, to learn the will of
God, and invoke His blessing on the undertaking.
Then, upon the 14th April, 1512, in presence of the
Emperor and his court, before princes, prelates, the
representatives of crowned heads, and the chapter
of the Cathedral, he proceeded to the opening of
the long-closed treasure chamber. Then was disclosed

---

* A profound reverence shrunk from the needless meddling with holy relics
It had been considered by Pope Gregory the Great to be irreverent and sacrilegi-
ous to seek to touch the bodies of saints, and relics were therefore left unmolested
in their shrines.

the "chasse" of wood and worked ivory (of which
Bishop Enen, an eye-witness, has already told us),
bearing its inscription, " The seamless Tunic of our
Lord and Saviour."

Having thus complied with the imperial desire
(as the same writer tells), the Archbishop trusted
that his anxious task was at an end; but, so far
from this, from every voice of that assembly uprose
a demand for the public Exposition of the Relic.
At length, overcome by their solicitations, and with
as little delay as the preparation for such a ceremonial
necessitated, the Archbishop, with solemn rite and
pageant, inaugurated the Exposition of the Holy Coat
for the veneration of the Faithful. The Relic remained
exposed during twenty-three days, during which time
it was visited by more than a hundred thousand
persons. The profound impression created in the
city and diocese, and the manifest fruits that resulted,
prompted the hope of a repetition at no distant date:
and eventually the Archbishop applied to the Holy
See for guidance in the matter, with what result
appears from the Bull of Leo the X. in 1515, in
which the Pope sanctions the solemn Exposition of
the Holy Tunic, at intervals of seven years,—the
periods to correspond with the Expositions at Aix
la Chapelle,—and further grants Indulgences to the
Faithful coming to venerate the Relic, under the

usual conditions. The observance, however, of these septennial Expositions soon fell into desuetude, owing to the frequent wars between France and Germany. Some few are known to have taken ·place, and there are records of the Relic having been on rare occasions shown to personages of the highest distinction.

Definite accounts are preserved of Expositions in 1531, in 1545 under Archbishop ¡John the IV. (Ludwig von Hagen), and in 1553. In the year 1585 a solemn Exposition was held, which lasted for three days— the 4th, 5th, and 6th of May—under Archbishop John the VII. (von Schärenberg). This festival appears to have originated by desire of the Papal legate, as ·a thank-offering for the peace : .and it is recorded that on this occasion Religious of the strictest closure were permitted to come and venerate the Relic. Another Exposition took place in 1594.

During the miseries of the thirty years' war, the city of Trèves was deemed to afford no sufficient security for the safety of the Holy Tunic ; and it was accordingly removed in secret to Cologne, in 1640. Here the Relic remained, until, on the termination of the war, it was brought back to Trèves, and solemnly exposed in 1655, under the Elector Archbishop Charles Gaspard. On this occasion the Relic was displayed *outside* the Cathedral, in a shrine attached to the western front. But fresh troubles arising, it was removed in 1667 to the fortress of Ehrenbreitstein, between which stronghold and its own city it appears to have passed and repassed many times in the course of years, according as its safety was imperilled by the constant wars.

During its different migrations, three Expositions are recorded as taking place at Ehrenbreitstein. In 1725, when it was privately shown to the Archbishop Elector of Cologne; in 1734, and in 1765, when it was exposed for a few hours in the market place on the 5th May. A circumstance in connection with one of these Expositions brings into prominence the precautions adopted to guard against any private or unauthorized interference with the Holy Relic. It appears, then, that not only was the shrine walled up with masonry, and the Sacred Robe itself enclosed in triple chests, but that each chest was furnished with three keys, only one of which was in the possession of the archbishop—the others being kept by the metropolitan chapter, who further had the right to be present at any opening or closing of the chests; as also to affix the great seals of the Chapter to the innermost chest. In fact the Chapter are known to have raised objections on the occasion of the Relic being exhibited to the Archbishop Elector of Cologne, in 1725; and they only gave way upon the express understanding that no private Expositions should be permitted in future.

A longer journey awaited the Relic in 1794, when, owing to the French Revolution, it was found necessary to convey it under trusted guardianship from Ehrenbreitstein to Würzburg, thence to Bamberg, and finally to Augsbourg, where it was secretly deposited in the chapel of the banished Elector of Trèves, Archbishop Clement Wenceslas. Here for a few years the Holy Coat remained, pending the dawning of the brighter times, which were to see it restored with jubilation to its home at Trèves.

THE EXPOSITION OF 1810.

With the advent of the year 1802,—when Trèves had welcomed back her bishops to dwell again in her midst, and when a new order of things seemed dawning on the world,—Bishop Charles Mannay was raised to the See of St. Eucharius; and among his earliest cares, the foremost appears to have been the recovery of the Sacred Tunic, still absent from its home and devoted people. Difficulties, however, were caused by the ruling powers of Bavaria and Nassau, but the good bishop (he was a Frenchman) was able to make interest with the Emperor Napoleon, through whose intervention all impediments were removed; and the Vicar-General Cordel was charged to bring the sacred Relic back to Trèves. His homeward journey is related to have been one long triumphant procession: everywhere the people poured out to greet the hallowed burden, as borne on car adorned with flowers and flags it traversed their districts—accompanied with joyful chants and hymns of praise—on its homeward route. At the church of St. Matthias it was received by Bishop Mannay, with his chapter, and conducted into the city through flower-strewn streets, and waving banners, midst the acclamations of the entire people. A public Exposition closed the bringing back of the Holy Tunic; and this lasted from the 9th to the 27th September. Now, for the first time, was the Relic shown upon the great marble tribune, behind the high altar, which had been erected by Bishop John Hugo in 1700. The numbers attending were computed at nearly a quarter-of-a-million. Wonderful cures were recorded; and the lasting conversions of multitudes, who had lived long years in vice and irreligion, testified to the success that had rewarded the Exposition—amidst the lawlessness and corruption which had been the natural outcome of the Revolution.

EXPOSITION OF 1844.

The course of the events detailed in this brief attempted sketch, has already brought us to our own century, and now leads to an event well within the memory of men of middle age. Plenty of the inhabitants of Trèves well remember the saintly and learned

Bishop William Arnoldi: they speak of him with affection, and hold his memory in high esteem and veneration. He was raised to the See in 1842 (it had been vacant for some six years before, since the death of Bishop Hommer), and upon his elevation he was everywhere met with earnest solicitations for the Exposition of the Holy Tunic, which had then been hidden more than thirty years. Need it be said— now that peaceful times had come—that the Bishop saw no grounds for refusing to comply with a desire in which he himself so warmly sympathized. Accordingly he fixed the 18th August, the feast day of St. Helena, for the inauguration of the solemn festival; and on the eve of the feast, the great bell, named after St. Helen (founded at the time of the Exposition of 1512), gave the signal, to be immediately echoed by scores of brazen throats from the towers of Trèves, for the solemnity of the day to follow.

The reports of eye-witnesses, still in the prime of life, whose memories vividly recall the event of 1844, agree to the letter in the details of that festal season; and their accounts are photographed as it were to the life in the chapter treating of it in the able work of Dr. Willems;—of which mention has been made, and to which the writer is indebted for so many details of this little narrative.

To give here their accounts in detail, would be in

effect to anticipate so much of the amazing spectacle the writer himself witnessed last month—September, 1891—that he prefers to give them place in the chapter to follow; but some special circumstances of the festival of 1844 must not be passed over.

On the 18th and 19th of August, the inhabitants of the city and its environs were to be the first to venerate the sacred Relic. Afterwards the crowds of strangers flocked to the city. Processions poured in from all sides; from the Dioceses of Mainz and Speyer, from Metz and Nancy, from Strasbourg and Cologne. From Luxembourg came 20,000 pilgrims, headed by their bishop and interspersed with innumerable clergy; these were received by Mgr. Arnoldi and his chapter, at the portals of the Cathedral.

Long hours and days of fatigue had many of them to undergo. Poverty, and the absence of means of communication, would compel the great majority to perform their toilsome journey not only in the *spirit*, but in the very *letter* of penitential pilgrimage. Eleven foreign archbishops and bishops came to venerate the Holy Tunic; and the long lines of pilgrims are dotted at intervals with the white cottas of their parish priests and clergy, who, bareheaded (as are all the men), alternate with the pilgrims the verses of psalm and litany.* The order preserved in the

* The entire numbers that passed before the Relic during the Exposition of 1844 are given as 1,100,000.

crowded city was something remarkable. Trèves at that time (without counting its environs) numbered scarcely more than 15,000 inhabitants; but here were sometimes 30,000 human beings arriving in one day. The wonderful decorum and tranquillity greatly impressed the French pilgrims. No police were to be observed, no sergeants de ville or national guard, and the troops were away at the manœuvres. " Who then keeps order ? " asked one of them. " A half-score of simple working men, detailed by the city authorities,— dressed in a distinguishable uniform, and bearing the Cathedral badge (the blood-red cross on field of white)— these are sufficient to indicate to all these crowds the way they should follow—the different churches to which they are assigned—from which, in regulated order, they will proceed to the Cathedral. All those crowds were their own police. It was a concourse of earnest-minded Catholics, a festival of believing Christians."

The days and weeks passed quickly by, with no check or mitigation of the ceaseless processions of pilgrims, that day by day defiled within the walls of Trèves ; nay, they rather increased as the time drew near for the solemn closing of the Exposition, which had been fixed for Sunday, 6th October, by which date it had lasted for a period of seven weeks. The results of the great festival were amazing, and far exceeded all the hopes and anticipations of Bishop

Arnoldi; nor can they be better described than in
some brief extracts from his closing address. "Scorned
and ridiculed," he says, "as this season has been,
I myself am witness, from intimate knowledge, of
the superabounding faith and piety which has raised
in God's sight a testimony which shall last to times
remote. . . . Nor have numberless miracles
been wanting. Of the greatest of these, the hidden
and spiritual ones, who can tell the numbers and
efficacy? The sinners of years converted during
these weeks of blessings; the tears of devotion, from
hearts well-nigh broken with sorrow; the good resolves,
the change of life, the acts of faith and hope and fervent
love, what miracles are like these? When I saw
young children in tears of joy and happiness, strong
men bowed down to earth, beating their breasts with
sighs and groans of contrition, I seemed to see before
these eyes the form of Him, who bore that Sacred
Robe, the Lord 'that doeth wonders,' visibly minis-
tering to the needs of fallen men. . . .

"And there have been physical miracles, too,—
an open sign that His right hand has not ceased
to aid His suffering people,—and the memory of
these will never be suffered to perish. Many have
been healed of their ailments; but many more who
were not healed have departed comforted, consoled,

and conscious of an extra power, to bear their sufferings for His will's sake.*

" Each day round about my dwelling, and each morning in this Cathedral, I seemed to see before me the Probatica at Jerusalem with its crowd of sufferers; whose mute confidence and trust could not have exceeded that of our own afflicted ones."

He concludes: " Now, God of my fathers, keep fast in Thy people this spirit, and ever incline its heart to Thine. I thank Thee for the countless miracles Thy grace has worked in this people's hearts; I thank Thee for the comfort, the consolations, the bodily cures accorded to them; but far above all I thank Thee for the numberless good examples Thou hast brought before their eyes in this blessed season. Hear, O Lord, my prayer, and ratify this my bene-diction."

" We cannot but believe," adds Dr. Willems, " that God has heard His faithful servant's prayer, and has preserved the spirit of faith in this people: nay, if a like solemnity shall never recur, we trust with confidence that its blessed fruits will still be found energizing in the hearts of His people, when Christ Himself shall come."

---

* A collection of the more notable cases of marvellous cures, submitted to searching scrutiny, and subscribed by eminent medical men, is preserved in the archives of the Cathedral in two large volumes. (See Appendix.)

F

CHAPTER VI.

In the opening chapter of this sketch reference has already been made to the preliminaries which preceded the Exposition of 1891, and, among these, to the long and searching scrutiny to which the Holy Coat was subjected by the Committee, presided over by Bishop Korum. Upon this matter, therefore, little need be added here.

The date of the opening ceremonial was fixed by the Bishop for the 20th August; and by the Brief of His Holiness Pope Leo the XIII., the Exposition was sanctioned for a period not to exceed two months: the same Brief recounts the Indulgences which were accorded to the Faithful attending the festival, and the conditions under which they were to be gained. Mgr. Korum next ordained a solemn Triduum of prayer, with Exposition of the Blessed Sacrament in all the churches for the three days immediately preceding the opening ceremony, and enjoined that the eve of the great solemnity be observed throughout the diocese as a day of abstinence and fasting.

Exposition of the Holy Coat, 1891.

The sketch of the ceremony of the opening day has been obtained from the accounts of eye-witnesses. By early dawn, on the 20th August, the city was already in commotion. Hours before the time fixed for the great function all Trèves was abroad, and the streets were thronged with men and women, of whom a very small percentage were likely, on this day at least, to gain admission to the Cathedral. The claims of their own people have of course to be considered first : the high city officials, the various corporations, guilds, the clergy and religious bodies, the various parishes, and religious and secular societies. At 9 a.m. the function commenced. Hours before, the body of the Domkirche had been crowded with an eager multitude, and now the huge chancel and sanctuary were equally thronged with ecclesiatics, high city officials, and Knights of Malta, in their old-world pageantry. Here the religious orders and congregations are represented by every variety of distinctive habit. The white wool of St. Dominic is conspicuous beside the brown tunic, cowl, and cord of St. Francis, and the grave and sombre robe o St. Benedict. Mingling with these, are seen the well-remembered habits of the sons of St. Ignatius and St. Philip (and of their English sons, too), not forgetting those of St. Alphonso and St. Paul of the Cross. Three prelates sit to the right of the altar, the Bishop of Luxembourg, our own Bishop of Birmingham (Dr. Ilsley), and Dr. Feiten, the Coadjutor Bishop of Trèves. Of clergy alone, between four and five hundred are present in the sanctuary to keep Trèves' festival.

And now the procession wends its way from the sacristy—cross bearer, acolytes, choir boys in their scarlet cottas, and seminarists. These are followed by a score or more of Maltese Knights, and a number of the guard of honour who shall be privileged to keep watch over the sacred Relic during its Exposition. Last, come the officiating clergy with the Bishop of Trèves, who is to celebrate the solemn Mass, which is to inaugurate the festival. They dwell for a short time at the east end of the nave, beside the magnificent case of relics which are here exposed — including, among other treasures, a nail of the Cross, large portions of the Cross itself, relics of St. Peter, St. Paul, St. Matthias, of the early saints and martyrs of Trèves, and many more ; and then, to the triumphant strains of the Vexilla Regis, the procession advances to the high altar. Thence the bishop and attending clergy mount the marble staircase to the tribune behind the altar, and, after a moment of silent prayer, the bishop removes the veil which had hidden the front of the reliquary, and the Relic of the Holy Tunic stands revealed to the eyes of the thousands within the old Cathedral walls, whilst the choir breaks out into the hymn from the Trèves Breviary, commencing:

> " O vestis inconsutilis
> Pro dulci nato virginis
> Arte parata textili
> Quis te sat ornet laudibus? "*

The bishop and assistants have meantime descended from the tribune to the high altar, and the Pontifical Mass begins. At the offertory the antiphon sung has reference to the festival, in the words:

> " O ter beata Treviris
> Lætare tanto pignore
> Christi togam
> Laudibus deprædica
> In sæculorum sæcula."

When Mass is ended, the Bishop advances, and in a short and fervent address reminds his hearers of the objects of the festival—to bring home to the hearts of men Him to whom the Relic referred, of whose life and sufferings it preached, of the unity of whose Church it was the symbol. "Laudamus Te, Christe, et benedicimus Tibi, quia per sanctam Crucem Tuum redemisti mundum."

At the request of the bishop all then left the

---

* The hymn and translation will be found in the Appendix.

Cathedral, excepting the occupants of the sanctuary, and these were engaged in passing before the Holy Relic and venerating it. At mid-day the first of the processions arrived from the neighbouring church of St. Gengulphus, and it was succeeded by those from other churches of the city.

At about 11 o'clock on the morning of the 23rd September, the writer and his son came in sight of the town of Trèves lying in sunshine, as the train from Luxembourg first crosses the silver Mosel. In that short glimpse the signs of Festa were apparent. The great tower of the Domkirche was hung with flags, and above them all waved the huge white banner with its crimson cross. Great now was the excitement of the country folk, with whom the train was packed, upon this first indication of the festival. Upon entering the station, the view of the platform thronged with travellers—penned in between wooden barriers, for safety's sake—caused some serious misgivings on the score of the probabilities of finding lodgment in the city, and seemed to justify the prudence of having remained at Luxembourg the previous night, rather than risk a late arrival at Trèves. But the crowd was too happy to be aught else than good-tempered; and so by degrees we worked a passage through the throng, and find ourselves at length in the open Platz. Here what a transformation since last year! On every vacant spot about the station yard are seen temporary wooden buildings, erected to minister to the wants of the thousands hourly arriving: extemporized cafés and restaurants occupy every vacant spot, and even the small front gardens are built over for the occasion. Lodging was evidently the first thing to be sought, so depositing our handy baggage in security, and disregarding the medley of tram-cars and other conveyances, we walked the short distance to the market square, close under the shadow of the grand Cathedral. This, it may be mentioned, is the better course for the traveller entering Trèves, if he would appreciate to the full the surprise which is in store for him. A walk of a few hundred yards along a very ordinary boulevard brings him to a turn in the road; and here, right close before his eyes, the grand pile of the Porta Nigra confronts him. Massive, blackened with age, but beautiful in its superb proportion, and towering to the height of ninety feet above the level of the pavement, the first encounter with this colossal ruin was to the writer one of the greatest surprises ever experienced; and though this had happened to him in the previous year, the feeling of breathless amazement was in no way lessened on the second visit.

With great misgivings of success, we made for

the Hotel Zum Dom, where the writer had stayed
the year before: and it was a positive tax upon his
credulity to be assured that he could have a room—
at double tariff certainly, but even on those terms
not immoderate in comparison with English hotel
experiences.

Now there was leisure to look about, and note the
signs of festival. On every side of the market square,
from the roofs and walls of the buildings, the flags
and banners show a blaze of varied colour. The
Papal white and yellow, with the red, white, and
black of the German Empire, show in greatest number,
but every variety of colour and design is found among
them: here is seen the figure of the Holy Coat
embroidered or painted on silk or bunting; here,
again, the figure of St. Peter, the Cathedral patron;
or of one or other of the early bishop saints who
once ruled the See. But everywhere is the Holy
Coat represented—illuminated on cards, reproduced
in photography, carved on articles of wood and ivory,
wrought in silver, gold, and baser metals, painted or
enamelled on porte-monnaies, card-cases, and pipes,
on match boxes and tankards, and impressed of course
on medals of every size and form. Then the vagaries
of commercial enterprise afford fresh cause for surprise,
for certainly one in every three or four shops displays
its objects of pious usage—its rosaries, medals, and

scapulars, its holy water stoups and devout pictures—however incongruous these may seem with the trade normally pursued. Not only at the booksellers, the print shops, the jewellers, and dealers in art objects,—which might be expected to minister incidentally to pious requirements,—but in the most unlikely spots, in the windows of the baker and butcher, nay, of the cheesemonger and chemist, room can be found for the display of objects of religious use.

Slowly working through the crowded market-square, we reach the church of St. Gengulphus, and here is plainly manifest that these crowds have come together for no mere purpose of holiday. The church is nearly full at mid-day: confessionals surround its walls, and on each of them a notice is prominently displayed of the languages in which confessions can be heard (thus, German, French, and Italian: or German, Flemish, and English). Each confessional has its group of penitents waiting their turn, and from early dawn till night—and late into the night—this has been going on, since the first opening of the Exposition. We pass from St. Gengulphus to the Jesuiten Kirche, and find the scene repeated; and the case is the same at the beautiful Liebfrauen-kirche, adjoining the Cathedral. If we had intended visiting the Holy Relic on this day, what we here saw would have deterred us till the morrow. Nothing could be more manifest than that all, or nearly all, the thousands who were flocking to the Exposition, *went first to the Sacraments*, and so prepared themselves for the visit to the august relic.

In the afternoon we work our, way through the crowded streets to the river's bank, and watch the interminable lines of procession coming in from the country, and crossing the old Roman bridge over the Mosel. Two by two they come on,—the monotony of the long unbroken line, varied here and there by the white robe of an ecclesiastic, or by some brilliant banner,—singing as they come, in alternate verse, the full-voiced chant of hymn and litany.

This is certainly a season of surprises, and the scene now witnessed is but one among many. To the most stolid Englishman, if he be a Catholic, the scene presented by a congregation at Mass or Benediction is perfectly intelligible, though perplexing to a stranger. The engrossment of each one in the objects of the faith, the disregard of all around, these find easy explanation. But here in the open roads and public streets is found a great multitude of men and women, whose religion is not confined to Sundays or the hours of church-time, but who in fields and streets can be occupied with prayer and praise, each regardless of the other—nay, rather, all bound together in the firm conviction of the common sense of the

work they are about. Here is no distinction of age
or sex. You see men and women, young as well
as old, strong-limbed peasants with their bronzed
faces, young men and boys, in whose look is no
suspicion of self-consciousness or false shame; who
have no idea that to say rosaries and chant litanies
in the streets of a city in the year 1891 can possibly
give cause for comment or surprise. The sight of
all these earnest, honest faces, the sound of their
hearty, ringing song, the absence of all effort at trying
to "look good,"—these ideas came to that stolid
spectator as a positive distraction to the edification
they gave, and were to him some such sort of
revelation as the first sight of ocean might be to
the eyes of the young child.

It is the early morning of Thursday, 24th September ;
the Jesuiten Kirche is crowded with worshippers, and
from half-past five o'clock Masses have been continuous, and Communion given every half-hour. At
the seven o'clock Mass the Communions alone occupied
fully twenty minutes; meantime the confessionals are
fully occupied, as indeed they are in all the churches
of the city. It would really seem as if the bishop
had impressed the services of the priests of half-a-
diocese for the needs of this single town during the
present season ; and we know that he had granted
full faculties to all foreign priests visiting the Expo-

sition, and that their offers of assistance were gladly accepted.

Time no more than sufficed to get back to the hotel for breakfast, and return to the church to be marshalled for the morning's procession, which slowly began to move away at about ten o'clock. It should here be observed that the greater portion of the Platz, at the west end of the Domkirche, had been surrounded by a wooden paling, enclosing an area of about two acres. Into this enclosure the procession enters, at a corner furthest from the front of the Cathedral, and in double file proceeds from end to end of the enclosure in serpentine fashion, so that by the time its leaders are at the Cathedral door the entire area is filled with a procession folded in ten or twelve coils. The object of this arrangement was to hinder all crowding and confusion, and to ensure the regular and unintermittent flow of pilgrims, who were continuously passing the Relic during the day. The actual distance from the Jesuiten Kirche to the Dom could be easily traversed in five minutes, so it will seem surprising that the time actually occupied from the door of the church to that of the Cathedral was close upon two hours, and this with scarcely any appreciable stand-still. No one seemed to find the time hang heavy; rosaries, hymns, and litanies at different sections of the interminable line fully occupied the attention of all, till each arrived at the western door of the Cathedral.

That portal passed, it is easy to imagine in what direction every eye was quickly lifted ; and the first glance brought a sense of assurance and content, for there, high up on the tribune above the high altar, surrounded by lights, the form of the Holy Tunic was plainly visible from the most distant corner of the church. The contrast, too, of the silence of the Cathedral (save for the footfalls of the moving line of figures) with the hum of prayer and litany without was surprising, and added to the sense of awe produced by the first glance at the sacred Relic, and the thought of all that it implied.

Passing np the south side of the nave and near the magnificent case of relics, of which mention has been made, the procession advances up the sanctuary, and at the Epistle side of the altar begins the ascent of the marble staircase. Here the double line merges into a single one, and thus one by one each person passes close before the seamless Tunic. On either side of the reliquary are stationed ecclesiastics, one of whom receives from each passer-by their rosaries or medals, and placing his hand through an aperture in the side of the reliquary, brings them into immediate contact with the hem of the garment, and then returns them to the owners. Each one tries to linger in passing, and eyes and heads are still inclined towards the Relic after they have passed. At just this juncture (should it be here confessed?) we two strangers took refuge in an angle formed by the marble columns, and let the procession pass on, (ourselves on our knees in partial concealment), and were able to remain unobserved for a few minutes; till at length on our being discovered we received a whispered intimation to "move on." Thus our English impatience of restraint had won for us an extra five minutes before the Holy Tunic—even if it had not served to enhance our country's credit for subservience to discipline.

After leaving the Relic the procession passed down the staircase on the Gospel side (at the foot of which some officials registered with a machine the number of those who passed), and left the building by the northern door; thence by a détour they reached the centre of the town, without colliding with the incoming processions.*

Thus closed, for the writer, a day which he hopes and believes will never lose its fresh hold upon his

---

* In consequence of an attempt made by a foreign priest to abstract a small portion of the sacred Relic, the bishop caused the following mandate to be affixed to the shrine of Exposition: "We, Michael Felix, by the grace of God and favour of the Apostolic See, Bishop of Trier, solemnly forbid the removal of even the smallest particle of the garment of our Lord Jesus Christ, at present exposed in this Cathedral, under pain of excommunication. Given at Trier, in our Episcopal Palace, 29th August, 1891. † Michael Felix, Bishop of Trier."

memory, as indeed he is confident that it will not
in the case of countless thousands who were privileged
to assist at this festival. But one further occurrence
is also associated with the day, which he is unwilling
to pass over in silence—the unexpected favour of a
most kindly interview with the Bishop of Trèves, in
which his Lordship expessed great interest in England
—spoke of the visit of the Bishop of Birmingham,
Dr. Ilsley, and also alluded to a former friendship with
his predecessor in that See, the late Dr. Ullathorne.
Mgr. Korum expressed surprise at hearing of the
advanced age of our own Cardinal Archbishop, and
smilingly observed that that quite exonerated his
Eminence from coming to venerate the Holy Coat.
He was also most courteous in imparting various items
of information, of which the writer has been able
to avail himself in these pages, and in putting him
in the way of obtaining further particulars of which
he was in search.

After the 24th September, but few days remained
to the closing of the solemn Exposition on 3rd
October. To outward appearance the city wore the
same festal look from day to day, varied only by the
differing numbers and nationalities of the pilgrims
daily arriving. The numbers increased greatly, as
the time of the closing drew near, as will be seen
by the daily table of attendance included in the

Appendix, and the highest number that passed the Relic was reached on Sunday, 27th September, viz., seventy-four thousand and ninety-three. On the more crowded days, in order that it might be possible for the multitude to pass before the Holy Coat, the bishop was compelled to prohibit the touching of the Relic with rosaries, medals, etc., as this necessarily delayed to some extent the flow of the procession, which already frequently lasted till after midnight. In the course of the forty-four days of the Exposition, seven hundred and thirty hours were occupied by the moving lines of pilgrims, an average of nearly seventeen hours a day out of each twenty-four.

For the first two hours of early morning the Cathedral doors were closed to the public, and only the sick and infirm admitted by a private door. These were received by the bishop in person, and to no other hands would he delegate the office of conducting them to the sacred Relic. They are brought up by twos and threes at a time—often having to be carried—and the bishop has taken his stand beside the Holy Tunic to receive them. Here he addresses each in touching words, urging on them conformity to God's will in regard to their infirmities. Now they are raised upon the low platform in front of the Relic : with trembling outstretched hands they touch the garment, and repeat after the bishop those very petitions which in the days of our Lord's ministry rose from the hearts and lips of suffering humanity—" Son of David, have mercy upon us"—" O God, help me"—" Lord, that I may see"—" Lord, if Thou wilt, Thou canst make me clean"—" Not my will, O Lord, but Thine be done." Eye-witnesses were moved to tears by the piteous longing gaze which the sufferers lifted towards the Sacred Tunic, with hope indeed, but with a hope tempered by humble resignation.

Certainly the arrangements for the season of Exposition had been prepared with the greatest forethought, and admirably were they carried out in detail. No point seemed to have been missed, no possible means of grace neglected. Mention has been made already of the copious facilities afforded to all for getting to the Sacraments. As a further aid thereto, Mgr. Korum had arranged for daily sermons at the Liebfrauenkirche—by twelve preachers selected by himself —upon the chief doctrines of the Faith, and the mysteries of the life of our Blessed Lord. Neither time, nor pains, nor prayers had been spared to render the festival a season of unusual grace and blessing for Trèves, for all Germany, and for the Church at large.

On all the Sunday mornings after the opening ceremony, Pontifical High Mass was celebrated at the Liebfrauenkirche, by one or other of the bishops who had come to venerate the Holy Coat. On August 23rd by Bishop Wahl of Dresden, Vicar-Apostolic of Saxony; on August 30th by the Archbishop of Cologne; on September 6th by the Bishop-Coadjutor of Trèves, Mgr. Feiten; on September 13th by the Bishop of Münster; on the 20th by the Bishop of Limbourg; on the 27th by the Bishop of Luxembourg; and on the 4th October, the closing ceremony, by the Bishop of Trèves.

These were but a few among the venerable archbishops and bishops who came, many from great distances, to venerate the Holy Tunic. Among the first to arrive were the Cardinal Archbishop of Vienna, and our own Bishop of Birmingham. Following these, came the Bishop of Providence (America), the Bishop of Ratisbon, the Bishop of Mainz, the Bishop of Ermeland, the Archbishop of Bamberg, the Archbishop of Cologne, the Bishop of Metz, the Chaplain Bishop of the Austrian Army, the Hungarian Bishop of Stuhlweissenburg, the Archbishop of Dublin, the Bishop of Cork, the Bishops of Strasbourg and of Paderborn, the Papal Nuncio, Mgr. Rinaldini, and the Bishop of Osnabrück. To these must be added mitred abbots, heads of religious orders, vicars-general, canons of cathedrals, and others of high ecclesiastical rank.

Of lay celebrities there was no lack, and if we

name but few among the multitudes of the noble
and high-born who attended the festival (and pages
might be filled with them), it is because, in sight
of Him who had worn that Robe, the worship of the
meanest of the pilgrims was no less acceptable. But
lest the faith and devotion which the Holy Relic
inspired, should seem to been restricted to the simple
and unlettered, the names of a few of the prominent
laity may be mentioned, as a sample of many others.
They are taken as they come, without reference to
rank or dignity—The Archduchess Maria Theresa
and daughters, Duke Paul of Mecklenberg and family,
Prince Merode, Marquis d'Encourt, Prince Löwen-
stein, Count Nesselrode, The Infanta of Portugal
and Princesses Anna and Theresa, Princesses von
Arenberg, Princess Salm, Count Merveldt, Count
von Stolberg, Count von Droste-Vischering (whose
sister was miraculously cured of paralysis at the
Exposition of the Holy Coat in 1844), Baron von
Schorlemer-Alst (a champion of the Church in the
German Parliament), Monsignore Stacpool from Rome,
Countess Stolberg, Sir Henry Bristowe, Marquis and
Marquise de Comillas Barcelona, Baron and Baroness
Koest, Countess Strall Dresden, Baroness Würzburg,
Duchess Maria of Mecklenberg-Schwerin, Princess
von Windischgrätz, Countess von Mocenigo, Arch-
duchesses Margaretha and Maria Annunciata, Countess

Metternich, Alderman Stuart - Knill of London, Baroness Olga von Leonrod, Baroness von Kettler, Marquis de Lambertye, etc., etc.

During the solemn Exposition no fewer than three hundred and fifty great foreign processions entered the city, of which some only of the more notable ones need be mentioned here.

One of the earliest processions, entirely of women from the city and suburbs, was organized by Bishop Feiten, formerly their much-beloved parish priest. At an early date, too, arrived a procession of 2,200 pilgrims from Metz, headed by their bishop, and their hymns and litanies were especially noticeable as being in the French language; to these the bishop made an address in French.* From Potch came 770; from Illingen 1200, with five superb banners. Next followed from Blankenheim 1000; from Cornelmünster 300; from Saarburg (Lothr.) 1000; from Sierck 1200; from Forbach 1200; from Kochern 700; from Dusseldorf 700; from St. Ingbert 1200. From Strasbourg, on 3rd September, arrived a procession of 800, with 40 priests. From the archdiocese of Cologne came in all 60 processions, three of which, from the city itself, contained 3600 persons. From the diocese of Luxembourg, between the 6th and 13th September, the various processions

---

* Mgr. Korum is a native of Alsace.

numbered 45,000. Then the dioceses of Speyer,
Lothringen, Limbourg, Münster, Osnabrück, Mainz,
Freibourg, Paderborn, and Strasbourg all furnished
their corresponding thousands. From America in
all came nearly 3000, and some few from Australia.
From Belgium came three large processions, that
from Arlon numbering 2800 persons. This amount
of detail may be considered sufficient for the purpose
of our sketch; to which it may be added, that the
English tongue was not unfrequently to be heard in
the streets of the city.

At length, with Saturday, 3rd October, arrived the
last day of the solemn Exposition of the Holy Coat.
At the hour of six p.m., when the doors of the
Cathedral were closed, 52,042 persons had passed
the Relic during that day; and from the opening of
the Exposition the grand total of the numbers represented 1,925,130 persons, nearly doubling those of
the last solemn Exposition in the year 1844.

After the closing of the Church, those who were
still inside—after passing before the Relic—joined in
five " Our Fathers," and in the antiphon, " Adoramus
te Christe, et benedicimus tibi, quia per sanctam
Crucem tuam redemisti mundum."

Sunday, the 4th September, saw the final ceremony
of the solemn Exposition of 1891. The Cathedral
was not opened till eight o'clock a.m., and within a

few minutes the entire building was crowded. The chancel was filled with clergy and civil authorities, and many of the notabilities above referred to were present, among whom were the Duke and Duchess of Mecklenberg, and the sister of the Emperor of Austria, the Archduchess Maria Theresa with her daughters. At nine commenced the solemn High Mass, the bishop being the celebrant; and upon its conclusion, the bishop and clergy bore away the Relic to a temporary resting-place, prior to its consignment to its permanent home, while the voices of the gathered thousands united in the hymn, "Grosser Gott, wir loben Dich."

At mid-day the Cathedral was again closed until three p.m., when it was once more crowded to excess for the bishop's final charge, of which the following is a meagre and unworthy abridgement. In the inspired words of St. John at Patmos, he begins : "Et vidi, et audivi vocem angelorum multorum in circuitu Throni, et animalium, et seniorum ; et erat numerus eorum millia millium, dicentium voce magna : Dignus est Agnus, qui occisus est, accipere virtutem, et divinitatem, et sapientiam, et fortitudinem, et honorem, et gloriam, et benedictionem."*

"Of this sublime vision of St. John, we have been permitted to see some reflex in the spectacle

---

* Apoc. v. 11, 12.

of the last few weeks. As he saw the Heavenly Jerusalem, so too our mortal eyes have seen the multitudes, in more than thousands of thousands, bowing down and crying " Worthy is the Lamb that was slain"—for was not this the burthen of the prayers, the hymns, the processions we have heard and witnessed?" He reminds his hearers that now they are met for one object—thanksgiving, for the Saviour's endless love, and for the mercies of this time of great graces. He describes their feelings as "made up of joy, thanksgiving, and hope. Of joy,—like the Bridegroom meeting the Bride,—of exultation in the Faith, at the close, too, of this unbelieving nineteenth Century,—a higher form of joy than the world's goods can give,—the joy of the soul stirred to its innermost depths, and made happy with the peace of Him to whom that garment once gave protection. Like the heathern emperor, they all might say, " Thou hast conquered, O Galilean'—conquered their hearts by the miracles of grace wrought through this blessed Relic—miracles greater far than those of the body, though these have not been wanting. Men came blind, and at their cry, ' Domine ut videam' (' Lord, that I may see'), their eyes were opened to the Faith of their youth." He tells how one afflicted man who came to touch the Relic, cried in his humility, "Oh! take my left hand, it is less guilty than the right.'

" Thanksgiving, again,—because, as in the Gospel story, 'they brought their sick from far and near, that they might touch the hem of His garment.' And *all* have received spiritual grace, if not all bodily cure. One writes : ' Though I have not been relieved of my complaint, yet, as I knelt before the Holy Tunic, I felt such joy, such consolation, that now I do not know whether my sufferings are not dearer to me than if I had recovered my health.'

" Thanksgiving, again,—for the actual bodily cures which God has deigned to work in an age of unbelief ; and hearty thanks, besides, to all those through whose agency these graces have been rendered possible— to the citizens who formed the guard of honour, and watched over the garment of their Heavenly King ; to the civic authorities ; and to the railway authorities for the ample facilities afforded even to the poorest, and for the vigilant care through which, under a merciful blessing of God, all had passed off without panic or accident.

And lastly of hope the bishop speaks. " What is our hope ? " he asks. " I am no prophet ; but whenever a great manifestation of faith has come uppermost, it has ever been the precursor of a new time—whether of suffering or consolation, who can tell ? But at least we are strengthened with a new grace ; and I confidently expect that this solemnity will be a landmark in the history of the Church—certainly of the Church in this diocese." The bishop next refers to the ancient custom of the " Laus perennis," the ceaseless praise formerly kept up in the religious houses, where, turn by turn, through day and night, the uninterrupted prayer and praise of God went on continually. " This we have seen again," he says, " each day bringing a new multitude—wave pressed on by wave, coming like a flood of living waters, and passing before the Holy Relic, praising the ' Lamb that was slain.' And when at night these voices were hushed, the guard took up their canticle of praise and prayer till morning came, and brought new worshippers. Let us continue," he concludes, " this eternal hymn of praise : let our grateful hearts never grow faint : let us here below intone the hymn to the Lamb who has saved us, so that one day we may continue it for ever in our eternal home."

In the evening, a remarkable demonstration of joy and gratitude occurred. The whole city was illuminated, and crowds surrounded the bishop's palace, whence they seemed unable to tear themselves. The full-voiced strains of hymns rose from that huge gathering, till at length, during a momentary lull, a voice called for prayers for their beloved bishop, when all uncovered and joined in fervently reciting five " Our Fathers," in gratitude to the Pastor, who, under God, had been the instrument of the blessings of their happy Festival.

Few more words are required to bring this short sketch to an end. Imperfect as the writer feels it to be, it may serve to suggest thoughts to some upon an unfamiliar subject, on which, too, much misconception exists. It does but propose to be, what it is called, *a sketch*, and that, far from complete. Those who may be anxious for fuller information, are referred to the works quoted in the Preface, or to a book by Fr. Beissel, S.J., " Geschichte des hl. Rockes," Trier, 1889, which may be said to summarize the pith of former writings. We may, however, shortly expect a volume from the pen of the Rev. R. F. Clarke, S.J., already foreshadowed by his admirable articles in the " Month" magazine.

But an answer to one question is sure to be expected : What about miracles ? And it is not yet the time to give the answer. That *many and various miracles have been wrought* during this Exposition is known to the favoured individuals, to their friends and relatives, and to the medical men and others on whom the task of verification devolves. Till this has been completed, the Bishop of Trèves and his chapter have everywhere discouraged the publication of details ; but so soon as the process of investigation has been closed, and the authority of science has confirmed, then, and not till then, will their complete history be made public.

To conclude is difficult, for how shall an obscure layman bring his brief story to an end without indulging in reflections which would come fittingly from his pastors, though unsuitably from him? He will make no such attempt. Leaving the moral for his readers to draw for themselves, he will, in conclusion, only presume to point to the story of an earthly king, the sight of whose robe had power to rouse the coward hearts of disloyal subjects:

" Kind souls, what! weep you when you but behold
Our Cæsar's vesture wounded? Look you here!
Here is himself, marred, as you see, with traitors."*

If men find a pathos here, may not the writer be pardoned this little essay upon the garment of the King of Kings?

---

* Julius Cæsar, Act iii., sc. 2.

POSTSCRIPT.

A CHAPTER on pilgrimages had been suggested to the writer, which he must be content to commute for a paragraph.

St. Jerome tells that from the time of our Lord's ascension to his own day (he died in 420), bishops, martyrs, and holy doctors had made proof that the choicest fruits of religion and divine science were only to be gained in their fulness by visiting the Holy Places.*

Thus much for the early Church. In the Church of to-day, the canonization of Benedict Joseph Labré makes known to this nineteenth Century that a life of perpetual pilgrimage to holy shrines may still, by divine vocation, be the means of attaining to heroic sanctity.

* Longum est nunc ab ascensu Domini usque ad presentum diem per singulos ætates currere, qui episcoporum, qui martyrum, qui eloquentium in doctrina Ecclesiastica virorum venerint Hierosolymam, putantes se minus religionis, minus habere scientiæ, nec summam ut dicitur manum accepisse virtutum, nisi in illis Christum adorassent locis de quibus primum evangelium de patibulo corruscaverat. (St. Jerom in Ep. Paulæ et Eustochii ad Marcellum. T. iv. p. 550. Ed. Ben.)

APPENDIX.

———

1. HYMNS FROM TRÈVES BREVIARY.

2. DAILY STATEMENT OF NUMBER OF PILGRIMS.

3. MIRACULOUS CURES AT FORMER EXPOSITIONS.

4. CHRONOLOGICAL TABLE.

5. LIST OF THE BISHOPS OF TRÈVES.

HYMN FROM TRÈVES BREVIARY.

O vestis inconsutilis
Pro dulci nato virginis
Arte parata textili
Quis te sat ornet laudibus?

Tu membra Christi contegens
Virtutem sumis inclytam,
Hinc fimbria morbos fugas
Fluxum-que sistis sanguinis.

Jesu cruorem roseum,
Nostræ salutis pretium,
Sacro bibisti vellere
Et flagellorum vulnere.

Te unitatis symbolum,
Te caritatis monitum,
Te noluit furentium
Manus secare militum.

Hæc sunt Eliæ pallia,
Hæc sunt Josephi licia,
Pro discolore murice
Tinxit Pilatus sanguine.

Qui te velatus claruit,
Nobis remittat debita,
Ut nunc amicti gratia
Post induamur gloria.

Deo Patri sit gloria,
Et Filio qui a mortuis
Surrexit, ac Paraclito
In sempiterna sæcula.

OFFERTORIUM.

O ter beata Treviris
Lætare tanto pignore
Christi togam
Laudibus deprædica
In sæculorum sæcula.

HYMN FROM TRÈVES BREVIARY.

(Translation by REV. R. F. CLARKE, S.J.)

O seamless Robe for Mary's child,
   By skilful fingers deftly done,
How can we praise thee as we ought,
   Robe of God's only Son?

Wondrous of old thy power to heal,
   Drawn from the sacred limbs of God;
Thy very hem dispels disease,
   And checks the flow of blood.

Thy sacred wool did drink the stream
   Which flowed to save from guilt and sin,—
The rosy blood that trickled down
   To wash poor sinners clean.

Thou art of unity the pledge,
   Symbol of perfect charity.
The rough fierce soldiers were afraid
   To rend thee shamelessly.

Elias' cloak was type of thee,
  And Joseph's coat of varied thread;
Instead of purple, 'twas with blood
  That Pilate dyed thee red.

By Him who wore thy precious woof,
  Be all our countless sins forgiven;
Through Him may grace adorn us now,
  Glory for aye in heaven.

To God the Father, glory be,
  And glory to the Eternal Son;
Glory, O Holy Ghost, to Thee,
  While countless ages run.

.Offertory.

In this thy pledge of love,
  Thrice happy Trèves, rejoice and sing;
As long as time shall last
  Proclaim the sacred Robe of Christ thy King.

DAILY STATEMENT OF THE NUMBERS PASSING THE RELIC.

August	20.	From noon till 11 p.m.	..	.. ..	24,600
,,	21.	,, 6 a.m. till 10-30 p.m.		.. ..	41,252
,,	22.	,, 6 a.m. till 9-30 p.m.		.. ..	37,846
,,	23.	,, 5-30 a.m. till 10-45 p.m.	..	..	44,300
,,	24.	,, 5-30 a.m. till 11 p.m.		.. ..	45,000
,,	25.	,, 6 a.m. till 9 p.m.	..	.. ..	42,000
,,	26.	,, 6 a.m. till 9 p.m.	..	.. ..	30,344
,,	27.	,, 6 a.m. till 9-30 p.m.		.. ..	31,042
,,	28.	,, 6 a.m. till 9-30 p.m.		.. ..	36,452
,,	29.	,, 5-30 a.m. till 9-30 p.m.	..	..	41,179
,,	30.	,, 5-30 a.m. till 11 p.m.		.. ..	47,286
,,	31.	,, 5-30 a.m. till 9-30 p.m.	..	..	36,347
September	1.	,, 5-30 a.m. till 10 p.m.		.. ..	45,000
,,	2.	,, 5-30 a.m. till 9-30 p.m.	..	..	45,625
,,	3.	,, 6 a.m. till 9 p.m.	..	.. ..	33,000
,,	4.	,, 5-30 a.m. till 8-30 p.m.	..	..	36,452
,,	5.	,, { 6 a.m. till 3 p.m. } { 6 p.m. till 9 p.m. }		.. ..	24,274
,,	6.	,, 5-30 a.m. till 9 p.m.		.. ..	33,500
,,	7.	,, 5-30 a.m. till 11-30 p.m.	..	..	38,830
,,	8.	,, 6-15 a.m. till 11-30 p.m.	..	..	40,282
,,	9.	,, 6 a.m. till 8 p.m.	..	.. ..	31,646
,,	10.	,, 6 a.m. till 9-30 p.m.		.. ..	30,051
,,	11.	,, 6 a.m. till 7-30 p.m.		.. ..	28,676
,,	12.	,, 6-30 a.m. till 9-30 p.m.	..	..	33,964
,,	13.	,, 6 a.m. till 11 p.m...		.. ..	39,312

September 14.	,,	6 a.m. till 11 p.m...	..	..	39,820
,, 15.	,,	6 a.m. till 11-30 p.m.	..	..	44,950
,, 16.	,,	6 a.m. till 11 p.m...	..	..	40,750
,, 17.	,,	6 a.m. till 11 p.m...	..	..	46,994
,, 18.	,,	6 a.m. till 10 p.m...	..	..	35,045
,, 19.	,,	(6 a.m. till 2 p.m.) (6 p.m. till 12 night)	..	..	35,521
,, 20.	,,	6 a.m. till 12 night	..	..	53,381
,, 21.	,,	6 a.m. till 11 p.m...	..	..	44,688
,, 22.	,,	6 a.m. till 11-30 p.m.	..	..	56,128
,, 23.	,,	6 a.m. till 10-30 p.m.	..	..	44,998
,, 24.	,,	6 a.m. till 10-30 p.m.	..	..	53,133
,, 25.	,,	6 a.m. till 11 p.m...	..	..	45,241
,, 26.	,,	6 a.m. till 12-30 night	..	..	59,223
,, 27.	,,	6 a.m. till 12-30 night	..	..	74,093
,, 28.	,,	6 a.m. till 12-15 night	..	..	58,678
,, 29.	,,	6 a.m. till 12-30 night	..	..	55,023
,, 30.	,,	(6 a.m. till 3 p.m.) (6 p.m. till 12-15 night)	..	..	49,316
tober 1.	,,	6 a.m. till 12 night	..	..	54,697
,, 2.	,,	6 a.m. till 1 a.m. ..	..	..	63,149
,, 3.	,,	6 a.m. till 6 p.m. ..	..	..	52,042

Total, 1,925,130.

MIRACULOUS CURES RECORDED OF FORMER EXPOSITIONS.

ALLUSION has been made to the miraculous cures worked during the Exposition in 1844. It may therefore be desirable to refer to some of the cures, which are stated to have been wrought by means of the Holy Coat on that occasion, as also at former Expositions.

In 1630 the Chapter of the Cathedral gave their written testimony to the fact that many miracles had been effected by the agency of the Holy Coat.

At the Exposition of 1655, various well-known cases of cures were named, which had occurred since the last solemn Exposition; and, indeed, it seems proved that although the periods during which the Relic has been exposed for public veneration, have been the most prolific in wonders, both spiritual and corporeal, still similar marvels have from time to time occurred,—though perhaps only in isolated cases, —from the mere propinquity of the Relic, in answer to the prayer of faith.

A notable case of the cure of a woman with an issue of blood,—similar, it would seem, to that related in the Gospels,—had occurred as far back as the Exposition of 1585, and had for those many years—up to 1655—been a matter of general notoriety, and a tradition of the diocese.

At the Exposition of 1810, the Vicar-General Cordel enumerates cases of paralytics, who had been carried to the church, returning to their homes unassisted and cured. Especial mention is made of an afflicted woman of Neunkirchen, Elizabeth Klein, aged 53, who had been for three years bedridden from gout. Upon the 14th September, she was carried into the Cathedral, and after some moments of prayer before the sacred Relic, was able to rise without assistance, to walk from the Cathedral, and join in the visits to the churches.

Of the miraculous cures which are believed to have occurred during the Exposition of 1844, we have already heard something from the then Bishop Arnoldi; and of these, naturally, more definite information is obtainable, as several accounts were written of them at the time, by men of note in the medical profession.

One, published at Luxembourg, details eleven cases of cures deemed to be unaccounted for by medical science. Another, published at Coblenz, describes twenty-three such cases. In a treatise by an eminent practitioner, Dr. Hansen, eighteen cases are selected from many others ; and of these he appends at length the reports and certificates he had collected from medical men, from the city authorities, clergy, and credible ocular witnesses. The mere headings of a sample of these are here given.

Countess of Droste-Vischering (before-named), age 19. Scrofulous affection of knee joints for three years ; dropped her crutches before the Relic, and walked from the Church, healed. After her cure a slight lameness remained, but she had no further need of crutches, nor of human assistance. Further, she who had herself been powerless, was enabled to join the Sisters of Charity, and devote her life to the care and assistance of the sick and afflicted.

John Michels, of Speicher, age 57. Cured of gout, 17 years' standing. This cure occurred on the occasion of a third visit to the Exposition of the Relic at Trèves, and he had in no way lost confidence, though his cure was not effected at the two former visits.

Marie Mentgen, of Neumagen, age 58. Ulcers on the breast, eight years.

Sœur Marie Angèle, Religious of Nancy. Spinal affection, which had lasted four years.

Rebecca Lamberz, of Cologne, age 34 years. Total loss of voice for a year.

Countess Louise de Villers, of Bourgesch, age 36. Nearly blind from ophthalmia, of 16 years' standing.

Anne Marie Schœmann, of Trèves, age 13. Deformed from infancy ; was seized with violent pains on touching the Relic, and could walk without crutches within two hours.

CHRONOLOGICAL TABLE

Of principal events in connection with the Relic, and with the
Cathedral Church of Trèves.

A.D. 40 (*circ.*). SS. Eucharius, Valerius, and Maternus sent by
St. Peter.

„ 67 (*circ.*). St. Paul sends Crescens to Gaul, who founds
churches of Metz and Mainz.

„ 312. Conversion of St. Helena.

„ 325. Council of Nicæa summoned by Emperor Constantine.

„ 326. St. Helena visits Jerusalem; sends relics to Trèves.

„ 527-566. Cathedral restored by St. Nicetius, after partial
destruction by the Franks.

„ 1016-1047. Cathedral renovated by Archbishop Poppo, after
invasion of Normans.

„ 1050. Visit of Pope St. Leo the IX. to Trèves.

„ 1147. Visit of Pope Eugenius the III.

„ 1152-1169. Archbishop Hillin.—Emperor Barbarossa.

„ 1196. Rediscovery of Holy Coat, and its deposition under
high altar by Archbishop John the I.

„ 1512. Diet at Trèves under Emperor Maximilian.—Exposition of Relic.—Archbishop Richard (von Griffenklau).
—Coadjutor Bishop Enen.

„ 1515. Bull of Pope Leo the X., authorising Expositions
every seven years, and granting Indulgences.

„ 1531. Exposition of Relic.

„ 1545. Exposition of Relic.

A.D. 1553.   Exposition of Relic.

,,   1552-1569.   Eastern Apse of Cathedral added by Archbishop Hillin.

,,   1585.   Exposition of Relic.

,,   1594.   Exposition of Relic.

,,   1640.   Relic removed to Cologne.

,,   1655.   Exposition at Trèves.—Archbishop Charles Caspar (von der Leyen).

,,   1667.   Relic removed to Ehrenbreitstein.

,,   1725.   Private Exposition to Archbishop Elector of Cologne at Ehrenbreitstein.

,,   1734.   Exposition at Ehrenbreitstein.

,,   1759.   Relic returned to Trèves.

,,   1765.   Relic removed to Ehrenbreitstein, and exposed on 4th May.

,,   1794.   Relic removed to Würzburg and Bamberg.

,,   1803.   Relic removed to Augsbourg, and concealed in chapel of Elector Prince Clement Wenceslas.

,,   1810.   Relic brought back to Trèves by Vicar-General Cordel. Exposition, 9th to 27th September. (Bishop Charles Mannay.)

,,   1844.   Exposition of Relic, from 18th August (Feast of St. Helena) to 6th October. (Bishop William Arnoldi.)

,,   1891.   Exposition of Relic, from 20th August to 3rd October. (Bishop Michael Felix Korum.)

"Ad multos annos."

BISHOPS OF TRÈVES.

1. St. Eucharius ⎫ Disciples	29. St. Paulinus 349-858
2. St. Valerius ⎬ of	30. St. Bonosius 358-373
3. St. Maternus ⎭ St. Peter.	31. St. Britonius ...373-386
4. St. Auspicius.	32. St. Felix II. 386-398
5. St. Celsus.	33. St. Mauritius II. 446
6. St. Felix I.	34. St. Leontius.
7. St. Mansuetus.	35. St. Auctor II.
8. Clemens.	36. St. Severus.
9. Moyses.	37. St. Cyrillus.
10. St. Martinus I.	38. Iamblichus.
11. Anastasius.	39. Evernerus.
12. Andrias.	40. St. Marus.
13. Rusticus I.	41. Volusianus.
14. St. Auctor.	42. St. Miletus.
15. Mauritius I.	43. St. Modestus 486
16. Fortunatus.	44. Maximianus.
17. Cassianus.	45. St. Fabitius 511
18. St. Marcus.	46. Rusticus II.
19. St. Navitus.	47. St. Abrunculus 527
20. St. Marcellus.	48. St. Nicetius......527-566
21. St. Metropolus.	49. St. Magnericus ..573-596
22. St. Severinus I.	50. Gundericus.
23. St. Florentius.	51. St. Sebaudus.
24. St. Martinus II.	52. St. Severinus II.
25. St. Maximinus I.	53. St. Modoaldus ..622-640
26. St. Valentinus.	54. St. Numerianus.
27. St. Agritius 319-332	55. St. Hidulphus....666-671
28. St. Maximinus II. 332-349	56. St. Basinus 671-695

104. Joannes VI.....1556-1567
(von der Leyen.)
105. Jacobus III. ..1567-1581
(von Eltz.)
106. Joannes VII. ..1581-1599
(von Schönenberg.)
107. Lotharius 1599-1623
(von Metternich.)
108. Philippus Christophorus
(von Sötorn.) [1623-1652
109. Carolus Caspar 1652-1676
(von der Leyen.)
110. Joannes Hugo..1676-1711
(von Orsbeck.)
111. Carolus Josephus 1711-1715
(von Lothringen.)
112. Franciscus Ludovicus
[1716-1729
(v. Pfaltz Neuburg.)
113. Franciscus Georgius
(v. Schönborn.) 1729-1756
114. Joannes Philipus
[1756-1768
(Reichsfreih von Walderdorf.

115. Clemens Wenceslaus
[Res. 1802
(Prinz v. Polen & Litthauen.)
116. Carolus........Res. 1816
(Mannay)
Sede vacante ..1816-1824
117. Josephus 1824-1836
(Ludwig Aloys v. Hommer.)
Sede vacante ..1836-1842
118. Gulielmus 1842-1864
(Arnoldi.)
Sede vacante ..1864-1865
119. Leopoldus 1865-1867
(Peldram.)
120. Matthias 13/11, 1867
(Eberhard.) bis. 1876
Sede vacante ..1876-1881
121. Michael Felix, Enthroned
25th September......1881
(Korum.)
"Ad multos annos."

CORRIGENDA.

PAGE 26—Footnote—*read* " Salmeron."

PAGE 35—line 18—*for* " troublesome " *read* "troublous."

PAGE 51—lines 18 and 19—*for* "at the same time" *read* " on the previous occasion, in 1810."

PAGE 67—line 12—*for* " Schärenberg" *read* " Schönenberg."

CHISWICK:
PRINTED BY PLATRIER AND SONS, HIGH ROAD.

www.ingramcontent.com/pod-product-compliance
Lightning Source LLC
Chambersburg PA
CBHW020752020726
47495CB00008B/2391